"I want you to say it."

Dragging his knuckles over her flushed cheek, he lowered his head until his lips hung a whisper above hers.

"Say what?" The mutinous line of her mouth wavered even as her muscles softened, bringing her pliant curves into sizzling contact with his hard planes.

"Say that you were glad I was here to take care of you today. How having me around was a good thing."

"I could've handled things just fine." She let loose a shocked gasp as he slid his palm up her spine, wrapped his fingers around her ponytail and gave it a sharp tug. "But I'm glad you were here so I didn't have to."

"Better."

The uneven cadence of her breath matched his as he covered her mouth in a deep kiss meant to remind her how they'd once burned up the nights.

* * *

How to Catch a Bad Boy by Cat Schield is part of the Texas Cattleman's Club: Heir Apparent series.

Dear Reader,

Every time I get to participate in a Texas Cattleman's Club series, it's so exciting. This book was no exception. I have never had as much fun writing a bad-boy story as I did with *How to Catch a Bad Boy*. Former professional polo player Asher Davidson Edmond may be many things—irresponsible, egotistical, sexy as sin—but he's no thief. Unfortunately, with all the evidence pointing to his guilt, he needs someone to believe in him. Too bad the one woman who could help him is the one he let get away five years earlier.

I love writing a strong woman of color, and Lani Li is a badass private investigator with something to prove and a padlock on her heart when it comes to her former lover. Too bad Asher's as sexy and charming as ever. These two were complete opposites of each other, and making them have to work together to figure out the mystery of the missing money was such fun.

I hope you enjoy this enemies-to-lovers bad-boy reunion romance.

Happy reading!

Cat Schield

CAT SCHIELD

HOW TO CATCH A BAD BOY

HARLEQUIN

DESIRE

Special thanks and acknowledgment are given to Cat Schield for her contribution to the Texas Cattleman's Club: Heir Apparent miniseries.

Recycling programs for this product may not exist in your area.

ISBN-13: 978-1-335-73510-2

How to Catch a Bad Boy

Harlequin Enterprises ULC
22 Adelaide St. West, 40th Floor
Toronto, Ontario M5H 4E3, Canada
www.Harlequin.com

Printed in U.S.A.

Cat Schield is an award-winning author of contemporary romances for Harlequin Desire. She likes her heroines spunky and her heroes swoonworthy. While her jet-setting characters live all over the globe, Cat makes her home in Minnesota with her daughter, two opinionated Burmese cats and a goofy Doberman. When she's not writing or walking dogs, she's searching for the perfect cocktail or traveling to visit friends and family. Contact her at catschield.com.

Books by Cat Schield

Harlequin Desire

Sweet Tea and Scandal

Upstairs Downstairs Baby
Substitute Seduction
Revenge with Benefits
Seductive Secrets
Seduction, Southern Style

Texas Cattleman's Club: Heir Apparent

How to Catch a Bad Boy

Visit her Author Profile page at Harlequin.com, or catschield.com, for more titles!

You can also find Cat Schield on Facebook, along with other Harlequin Desire authors, at Facebook.com/HarlequinDesireAuthors!

To Bri and Ella.
Thanks for all your support so
I could get this book written.

One

Asher Davidson Edmond lay on the jail cell's hard bunk, arm thrown over his eyes to block out the gray concrete walls and dingy ceiling. How the hell had he gotten here? Correction: he knew how. A police escort in the back of a cruiser. As to the chain of events that had landed him in this mess, he'd been completely blindsided.

Despite some of the risky behavior he'd demonstrated in his thirty-one years, he'd never imagined landing behind bars because of something he hadn't done. And he definitely *hadn't* been embezzling funds from the festival. He might've bent or even broken a law or two in his youth, but that had been petty stuff. Stealing for his own gain was the last thing he'd do.

"Hey, rich boy."

The mocking voice belonged to the blocky, muscular

cop who'd escorted him back to his dank, windowless cell after his arraignment. Asher's molars ground together at the man's taunt. Apparently, he'd gone to high school with Deputy Vesta's younger sister and hadn't treated the girl too well. He had to take Vesta's word for it because he didn't remember those teenage years all that well. Something about laughing at her when she'd asked him to prom… Not one of his finest moments, obviously.

"Yeah?" Asher responded, not bothering to move. Quashing his jittery emotions, he packed as much sardonic boredom as he could into the single word, all too aware that he wasn't doing himself any favors by acting like a jerk. Still, nothing would change Vesta's rock-solid perceptions of him, and after years of coping with his adopted father's nonstop disapproval, he reflexively retreated into behaving like a sullen, entitled prick.

"You've got a visitor."

Hope exploded in Asher's chest.

Had Ross and Gina changed their mind about his guilt after failing to support him at yesterday's bail hearing? While his siblings' abandonment had aroused panic and uncertainty, Asher had known better than to expect his adopted father to show. Nor did he expect Rusty Edmond had come to see him now, unless to drive home his acute regret for adopting his second wife's son.

Asher had his own complaints on that score. Why had Rusty bothered with a legal connection when he'd never truly embraced Asher as one of his own? Or maybe he had—the man demonstrated little affection toward either of his biological children and between criticizing Ross's abilities and dismissing Gina's talents, none of the Edmond offspring had a great relationship with him.

That hadn't stopped Asher from spending his teen years fighting an uphill battle to win Rusty's affection though. And when all his efforts had failed, Asher had begun acting out. If he couldn't win his stepfather's approval, then he figured he would become truly worthy of Rusty's disdain.

Yet as difficult as his relationship with his stepfather was, Asher's connection with his stepsiblings was as close as if they were blood relations. Ross had been twelve and Gina ten when fifteen-year-old Asher had come to live with them. He'd enjoyed playing big brother to the pair and the trio had bonded immediately. Even though Rusty had only been married to his mother for three years, they'd been formative ones for all three kids and they'd remained tight even after Rusty and Stephanie divorced and Asher headed off to college.

Which was why the silence from the Edmond siblings was so ominous. Since his arraignment, he'd consoled himself by speculating that Rusty—intent on teaching his adopted son a lesson—had barred Ross and Gina from showing up in court. But as the hours stretched out and he'd not heard from either of his siblings, Asher started to worry that they believed he was guilty and had turned their backs on him.

Unrelenting panic swelled in his chest. At the arraignment he'd learned the charges against him were worse than he'd been led to believe. It wasn't just the theft of the funds—that could've been handled locally—but the money had disappeared from the banks, sent by wire transfer and that meant the feds were involved. Even if he'd wanted to, Rusty couldn't use this as a teachable moment for his adopted son and make the charges go away.

Asher was in *deep.*

With his bank accounts frozen thanks to the embezzlement charges, he hadn't been able to post his own bail. Naturally he'd hoped that his family would believe that he'd never do anything like what he'd been accused of and help him out. But as the hours passed, his despair had grown. Only now it appeared as if he'd been worried for nothing. One or both of them had decided to help him out.

"You've got five minutes," Deputy Vesta said, his tone brisk.

Asher sat up and blinked in the sudden brightness. As his eyes adjusted, he focused on the person standing on the other side of the bars. The individual was neither his tall, lanky brother nor his stylish sister, but a petite woman in figure-hugging jeans and high-heeled boots, her long black hair slicked back into a neat, low ponytail. Probably another fed come to pick at him about the missing funds.

But then she stepped closer and he glimpsed her features.

"Lani Li?"

He could barely breathe as recognition landed a sharp jab to his gut. Then he rallied and pushed to his feet, fighting to remain upright as his emotions executed a wild swing between delight and confusion at her appearance. Had she heard about his plight and come rushing to help him? His heart hoped so. It thumped hard against his ribs as he processed his outstanding luck.

However his euphoria dissipated as he noticed the glower in her mink-brown eyes. Spots of color flared in her cheeks, marring the uniform perfection of her pale skin. She'd compressed her luscious lips into a flat line that broadcast her disdain and the only thing keeping her arched brows from touching was the bottomless vertical indent between them. To say she looked less than pleased to see him was an understatement, but putting aside his desperate need for rescue, her arrival flooded his mind with vivid, racy memories.

Until she spoke…

"Asher." Her tone was all business.

"What a surprise," he murmured, advancing toward her, drawn like a bee to a flower.

Her scent hit him before he wrapped his hands around the bars and leaned in. She smelled like warm vanilla and spicy cinnamon, all lush sweetness and mouthwatering delectability. He remembered burying his nose in her hair and drawing her unique perfume into his lungs. How she'd tasted like sweat and sunshine as they'd made love beside a raging river, crushing pine needles beneath their straining bodies and releasing the astringent scent. The simple act of breathing her in now slowed his heart rate and soothed his restless nature.

"What's it been?" he continued blithely. "Five years?"

She gave a curt nod. "About that."

"Long time."

"Yep." Lani narrowed her eyes and scanned him from the top of his close-cropped brown hair to the toes of his brown Berluti loafers. "You look like hell."

"Well," he drawled with a lazy shrug while his brain scrambled to process that she was standing there. "I have been locked up in here for a day and a half, so…"

While finishing the sentence, he trailed his gaze over her, following the buttons of the white button-down shirt she wore beneath a practical navy blazer, over the swell of firm breasts and the flat plains of a taut abdomen to the waistband of the dark denim. He knew that body. He *adored* that body. Curves in all the right places. Honed muscle beneath silky soft skin. He'd spent long hours guiding his lips and hands over every inch, learning what made her shiver, moan and whimper.

"You look really great," he drawled, recalling that time he'd nipped the firm mound of her perfect butt and made her squeak in surprise. "So, what brings you by?" Asher posed the question lazily, chatting her up as if they'd bumped into each other at a barbecue rather than a jail cell. One corner of his mouth kicked up as he delivered a smoky look her way.

"I've gotta say, you're the last person I expected to see here."

"I'm on a case," she told him.

"I'm intrigued. Care to tell me about it?"

"I'm investigating the theft of the festival funds."

"Who do you think did it?" he asked.

She cocked her head and shot him an incredulous look. "You."

"So, you're on the Asher-is-a-thief train." He nodded, unsurprised by her answer. "I thought you might believe I was innocent."

With a long-suffering sigh, she swept aside her blazer and set her hand on her hip. The gesture exposed an empty holster clipped to her belt. He stared at the tell-tale harness as lust blindsided him. The thrill wasn't entirely sexual. Since he was a kid, Asher had lived for the next great adventure and had spent most of his twenties chasing anything exciting or dangerous. The thought of Lani packing heat turned him on in so many ways. His skin tingled and the tips of his fingers began to buzz with the need to touch her.

"Looks like you became a special agent after all," he said, his gaze drifting up her torso, pausing momentarily to revisit the enticing curve of her breasts before making contact with her hostile glare. "What are you? FBI? ATF? DEA?"

Her sooty eyelashes flickered. "I'm a private investigator."

"You don't say." This intrigued him.

Lani had been on the cusp of attending graduate school when they met five years earlier and planned to study criminal justice. She'd graduated college with a degree in sociology and a passion to make the world a better place. Despising injustice, she'd decided a career in federal law enforcement would offer her the best chance to make a difference.

"Well," he continued, "get me out of here and you can do all the private investigating you want."

Even before her eyes flared in outrage, Asher regretted flirting with her. She was the only person who'd come to see him and he was treating her like some random chick he'd met at a bar instead of the dazzling prize he'd foolishly let slip through his fingers.

Her full lips, bare of lipstick, puckered as she let an exasperated breath escape. As if they'd last kissed yesterday instead of five years ago, he recalled how her lip balm had tasted like strawberries. How her long silky hair had tickled the back of his hands as he'd drawn her close. From their first kiss to their final heartbreaking embrace, he hadn't been able to get enough of her.

"You're still the same frat boy, aren't you?" Her words splashed icy water on his libido.

"I'm not."

The nickname stung the way it had five years earlier. They'd met while she'd been employed as a waitress on Appaloosa Island in Trinity Bay off the coast of Texas. He'd been lazing around before what had turned out to be his final season playing professional polo. Intrigued as much by her brilliant wit as her killer body and gorgeous face, every time he ate at the resort's restaurant, he'd made sure to be seated in her section.

To his chagrin, nothing about him had charmed her. Unimpressed with the giant tips he'd left her, she'd sized him up as idle and aimless and dubbed him "frat boy" even though he'd left college behind half a decade earlier.

"These days I'm the vice president of operations in charge of The Edmond Organization's Bakken business." He puffed out his chest, wondering if he could impress upon her that he was serious and successful, someone who had a plan and stuck to it instead of roaming around the world chasing one polo season after another.

Although his practiced tone was one of pompous confidence, it didn't reflect his true feelings. In fact he hated the endless dull details demanding his attention and made the barest effort to manage his team.

He'd been with the company for a little over nearly two years, bullied into taking the position because Rusty was tired of subsidizing Asher's "unproductive life-style" and threatened to cut off all support unless Asher did something to earn the money.

"Yet you're barely ever in the office," she said, her skeptical expression indicating she'd already heard an earful about him.

"I've been busy with the Soiree on the Bay festival." An exaggeration. He'd had little to do with the practical aspects of organizing the luxury food, art and wine extravaganza.

"Yes," she murmured dryly, "that seems to have led to your current state of incarceration."

As much as Asher wanted to argue, what could he say? The steel bars blocking him from freedom said it all. Nor could he point to anything he'd done since they'd parted ways that would meet with her stringent standards. She was one of the most focused and task-oriented people he'd ever met. From the beginning she made it perfectly clear that his lack of ambition frustrated her. In every way that mattered, they were opposites. Yet he was drawn to her by an undeniable hunger that proved as distracting as it was intoxicating.

While it might have been her striking looks that first attracted him to her, what inflamed his pursuit in the face of one rejection after another was her courage, un-flinching strength of character and no-nonsense out-look.

And he loved a challenge.

Her aloofness fired his determination to discover the woman hiding behind her prickly exterior. Yet as satisfying as the chase had been, catching her had surpassed his wildest dreams. Nor had his attention shifted to his next conquest after getting her into bed. She'd proved to be more exhilarating than any woman he'd ever known. And through the course of their whirlwind affair, she'd had a profound effect on him.

During those blissful summer months, he'd become someone…*different*. Someone who stopped joyriding through life and started to question his purpose. Someone who considered another's hopes and desires might be just as important as his own.

Yet it couldn't last. They were heading down two completely different paths. She was off to graduate school in the fall, destined to make something of herself. Faced with losing her, he'd relapsed into the aimless, restless, the unreliable "frat boy" she'd christened him. And often in the intervening years, he'd wondered what would've happened if he'd been a better man.

Lina raised a slim black eyebrow and shook her head. "Do you have any idea how much trouble you're in?"

Her stony demeanor brought him back to the predicament facing him. "I'm starting to," he grumbled, his panic surging once more. If he could only get her on his side… "It's all a huge misunderstanding."

"Is it?" she countered. "The evidence against you is pretty damning. Millions are missing from the festival accounts and all the withdrawals appear to be in your name."

"I swear I didn't steal a single cent."

For days Asher had been denying any knowledge of where the money had disappeared to. No one believed him. Not his family. Nor the authorities. He appeared responsible, so everyone believed he was guilty.

"I've talked to the investigators," Lani went on as if she hadn't heard Asher protest his innocence. "There were payments made to a tech firm, a music company, a luxury jet charter enterprise. Many of the transfers seemed as if they could be legitimate, but the companies don't exist and money was siphoned out of the accounts as soon as it was put in."

This was more information than he'd previously heard. Fake corporations with real bank accounts. That sort of thing took calculation and finesse. And if anything pointed to Asher's innocence, it was that his planning skills were subpar, just ask his team at The Edmond Organization.

While he'd been mulling his shortcomings, Lani's gaze rested heavily on his face, her expression grave and expectant. "No one has any idea where the money is now."

"Me included." Heat flared in his face as frustration bubbled up inside him. It was one thing for the Edmonds to believe his guilt, but he needed Lani's help if he was going to get out of this mess. "I didn't take any of it."

Unfazed by his continued denials, she continued to assess him with cool detachment. "There's a condo in the Maldives with your name on it."

"It isn't mine." Anger flared. Where was all this damning evidence coming from? With the money trail leading directly to him, was it any wonder no one believed his innocence? "I don't even know where the Maldives is."

"It's an island off the coast of India." She paused and

studied him through narrowed eyes. "More importantly, there's no extradition treaty with the US."

"Meaning I intended to take the money and run."

He barely restrained a wince at her obvious disgust. *Damn.* As hard as it had been to glimpse the betrayal and disappointment on his family's faces as he'd been escorted out of the Edmond headquarters in handcuffs, the scorn rolling off Lani cut even deeper. He'd never admit it, but once upon a time he'd wanted to be her hero. Obviously his need for her admiration hadn't dimmed.

"I'm telling you that I didn't steal any of the festival's funds and I didn't buy a condo in the Maldives." Asher gave his head a vigorous shake. "I didn't do this. Why won't anyone believe me?"

Lani glared at Asher, unable to believe that five minutes ago, as she'd walked through the door leading to these jail cells, she'd been besieged by an attack of butterflies—*butterflies!*—at the thought of seeing him again. She braced her will against the pull of his striking good looks, broad shoulders and overwhelming masculine appeal and cursed the part of her that revisited the bliss of his hard body surging into hers and the peaceful aftermath snuggled against his big warm chest. The double-barreled shot of mind-blowing sex and tender romance had torn her defenses apart.

She'd spent the last five years putting her walls back up. Yet when it came to Asher Edmond, she always underestimated his charisma. Her throat clenched. She remained as woefully susceptible to him as ever. At least she hadn't let on how her heart had leaped at her first glimpse of him. Or given any hint of how she'd rushed from a client meeting with the famous musician Kingston Blue, to this jail cell in Royal, Texas, breathless and giddy and all too aware that this new case would bring her into close proximity with Asher once again. Last time she'd almost ruined her life because of him. She must *not* be led astray again.

Recognizing that she was grinding her teeth, Lani unlocked her jaw with an effort. "If you didn't do it, then who did?"

"I have no idea."

His denials didn't surprise her. Given the serious charges facing him, Asher would be a fool to admit wrongdoing. At least not until his lawyer had plea-bargained his sentence down for cooperating with the investigation.

"It would be good for you if the money was returned." A pause. "I could help with that." Kingston Blue wanted answers. She intended to get them.

"If you think I have a clue where the missing funds have gone, then you're going to be disappointed."

"When it comes to you," she retorted without considering her words, "I'm used to being disappointed."

For a second he looked stricken and Lani wished she'd guarded her tongue.

"What I mean is…" Rummaging through the ashes of their brief romantic fling to dig up all the old hurts and disappointments was not the way to get him to trust her. "Look, I'm here to do a job. I'm not here as your friend. We had a lot of fun that summer, but let's not pretend that we ever intended on seeing each other again once we parted ways."

Asher winced. "I'm sorry for how things ended between us."

Lani scoured his expression to determine if he truly felt remorse or if he was merely spouting more of his pretty words. *Fool me once...*

"Don't give it another thought." She pressed her lips into a grim line. The man already thought too much of himself. Why give him an inkling that their breakup had bothered her at all? "I haven't."

That summer everyone had warned her about him. She should've listened, should've followed her initial gut instincts and steered clear. Especially after her parents voiced their disapproval of their relationship when Lani had started reconsidering whether she should head to graduate school as planned or take a gap year and spend the time with Asher. She'd been such an idiot to think he'd been at all serious about her.

"I know I was a bit of a tool back then," Asher said as if she hadn't brushed off their fling as inconsequential. "But those days are behind me. I'm not that guy anymore."

His reputation said otherwise. He had an active love life, playing as fast and loose with women's hearts as he had with the festival's bank accounts. Every social media post featuring him should be captioned *#heartbreaker*.

"Forgive me if I have a hard time believing that given that you're behind bars at the moment."

"Like I said, I'm innocent." A muscle ticked in his jaw. "I was set up."

Don't be taken in by his earnest denials. Lani steeled herself against the agony in his intense brown eyes, but couldn't quell the sudden frantic pounding of her pulse.

His silver tongue had drawn her in all those years ago and she'd almost given up her dreams to be with him. She just couldn't allow a lapse in judgment to happen again.

"Do you have any evidence of being framed? Or a theory who might be involved?" When she spied the way his chiseled lips thinned in frustration, Lani nodded. "That's what I thought."

For a long moment they stared at each other and Lani couldn't decide if she wanted him to be innocent or guilty. For his sake, the part of her that had once loved him hoped that he had been set up, but the heartbroken portion needed him to be a bad guy. Since they'd parted, she'd been telling herself that she was better off without him. Misery loomed if she stopped believing that.

"I guess that's it then. Your mind is made up. There's nothing more I can say to convince you." He looked so despondent that Lani's heart contracted in sympathy. "Well, it's been really great catching up with you. Good luck with the investigation."

Crap. Well, she'd done an outstanding job of alienating him before learning anything. "If you're innocent, you could use…help." She couldn't bring herself to say *my help.* Sucking in a steadying breath, she tried again. "My client wants me to find the money…"

"Did my father hire you?" Asher looked hopeful. "He was very impressed by you back when we dated. In fact, his only criticism was why a woman with your brains and ambition would waste your time with me."

"My client would prefer to remain anonymous."

Which wasn't true. Kingston Blue had given her no

such instructions, but she was here to get information, not give it out.

The musician had agreed to perform at Soiree on the Bay and, like many people, he was out a lot of money thanks to Asher's embezzlement. Kingston Blue had deep pockets and wasn't in any desperate financial straits, unlike many of the vendors and attendees of the aborted festival, but he was a savvy businessman who didn't take lightly to being swindled. He'd met the entire Edmond clan and was quite convinced that there was more to the story than Asher Edmond acting alone to defraud all the people who'd put money into the festival.

Lani had been surprised when a high-profile client like Kingston Blue had contacted her about the case, but it became clear right away that the singer had done his homework and knew all about her connection to Asher Edmond. Kingston also knew that their fling hadn't ended amiably, at least not on Lani's part.

Professional ethics prompted her to warn Kingston that her prejudice against Asher might affect her work, but the musician believed her familiarity with the family made her the perfect person to investigate them and find the money. After the first obvious leads had panned out, progress had stalled on discovering the bulk of the missing funds. The feds had stopped investigating other suspects once all the evidence solidly pointed at Asher.

Despite her misgivings, in the end, the outrageous retainer Kingston offered was too tempting to resist. Plus, a check in the win column would open the door to other prominent clients. This case was the gateway to turn her fledgling business into the most sought-after investigative firm in Dallas.

But first she had to find the money Asher had stolen and for that she needed his cooperation.

"Sure. Okay. I understand." Asher raked his fingers through his short dark hair. "But when you see my dad, tell him I've learned my lesson. It would be great if he could bail me out now."

Lani saw no reason to correct Asher's assumption that his father had hired her. If he believed that Rusty wanted him to cooperate with her investigation, all the better.

"Let me go see what I can find out about that," she said, suddenly eager to escape.

Asher stared at her intently, his gaze growing ever more piercing as the seconds ticked by. Heat flared beneath her skin at the intensity of his stare. His look wasn't sexual in nature, yet she'd always been so aware of his body and keyed into his moods. She saw now how longing and relief mingled in his expression as he believed, perhaps for the first time since his arrest, that someone might be willing to stand in his corner and believe in him.

"Thanks."

"Don't thank me." She needed to find the money. He was her ticket to do that. "I'm on a case. I think you can help me with it. That's all. Don't read anything more into it."

"Sure. Whatever you say." His even, white teeth flashed in a relieved grin as she turned to go. "And, Lani…"

She hated the way her heart spasmed as she headed

for the exit. The powerful lure of their shared history was a stronger temptation than she'd expected. But she couldn't let herself be ensnared by her longing for him. He'd been bad for her back then, and he'd be even worse for her now.

"Yeah?" Standing before the door, waiting for the buzz that would indicate it was unlocked, she made the mistake of glancing Asher's way.

A smile of genuine delight lit up his brown eyes and softened his lips into sensual curves. "Seeing you again is the best thing that's happened to me in a long, long time."

The buzz sounded. Without uttering another word, Lani yanked open the door with far more force than necessary and left. She collected her phone and keys from the deputy guarding the cells, and then she was run-walking through the police station and stepping out into the blistering hot August afternoon. She didn't stop moving until she'd reached her SUV in the parking lot. Breath coming in ragged gasps, she bent forward and set her hands on her knees while the blood pounded in her ears.

As her pulse slowed, she unlocked her vehicle and slid behind the wheel. She couldn't do this. Pulling out her phone, she began to scroll through her contacts in search of Kingston Blue's name. To hell with the money or the boost to her reputation this case offered, working in close contact with Asher was going to mess with her emotions again.

"Lani," Kingston's smooth deep voice soothed her ragged nerves. "I didn't expect to hear from you so soon. Did you meet with Asher Edmond?"

"Yes." She searched for a way to extract herself from the case without damaging her credibility. "He claims he's innocent."

"Do you think he is?"

Did she? "The evidence suggests he's guilty."

"But you know the guy. What's your take?"

"It's all a little too obvious." Lani didn't realize this fact had been bothering her until right now. "Asher isn't stupid or naive. How could he possibly think he could get away with it?"

"So, you agree that there's something more going on."

"Maybe. I don't make assumptions this early in a case."

"Fair enough." Despite Kingston's neutral tone, his inflection reflected disappointment. "So what's your next step?"

"Well, having Asher behind bars makes getting information from him about the festival bank accounts nearly impossible, and since the feds froze his assets and his family isn't stepping forward to help, it doesn't look like he can make bail."

"If I put up the money to get him out, I'm counting on you to make sure he doesn't run. That means he's your responsibility twenty-four/seven."

"That's…"

Impossible. Outrageous. Too much to expect from her.

She couldn't handle that much contact with Asher. There had to be another way. Yet even as she scrambled for a logical excuse to give Kingston, she knew there was only one answer.

"Doable."

"Great, then get me the details so we can get his bail paid and let's hope our boy can lead you to the missing money."

Two

Confronted with spending another miserable night cooling his heels in jail, Asher set aside his dinner of a roast beef sandwich, snack-size bag of potato chips and fruit cup. No doubt refusing the simple fare would be perceived as snobbishness, but in truth, the acid churning in his stomach left him unsure if he could keep anything down.

"Your bail's been posted," Deputy Vesta said in clipped tones as he unlocked the door to his cell.

Asher lacked the energy to hide his overwhelming relief as he pushed to his feet and approached the opening. "Was it my dad?"

Even though Lani hadn't confirmed that Rusty had hired her, he was leaning into the hope that his father had come around to believing his adopted son was innocent.

Vesta scowled in disgust. "Do I look like I care?"

No doubt the deputy—along with most of the town—believed he deserved to remain permanently behind bars and was disappointed at this turn of events. Suspecting further questions would irritate Vesta further, Asher kept his mouth shut. Per the terms of his release, he was fitted with a court-mandated ankle monitor and instructed about the rules surrounding his release.

After collecting his belongings, he stood in the police station lobby while the public defender assigned to his case talked on the phone. Asher peered through the glass front door into the golden sunshine of early evening, wondering who had paid his bail and when they would show up to give him a ride back home.

His spirits rose as he spied his sister approaching the police station entrance. Gina was looking at her phone as she pushed through the door and didn't see him until he greeted her.

"Gina, hey," Asher called. He stepped forward to intercept her, his arms open wide. "It's great that you're here. I'd almost given up on anyone coming to pick me up."

"You're out?" Gina stopped dead, and then actually backed up several steps and cast her eyes around frantically as if desperate for someone to rescue her. "How?"

"You paid my bail…?" Asher trailed off at her headshake. "Well, *someone* did. Maybe it was Ross?" Doubts began to close in when she continued to look panicked and confused. "Or dad. I think he hired an investigator to help find the missing money."

Asher trailed off as his sister's knuckles whitened on the hand that clutched her purse strap. The strain she'd been under these last few weeks was fully evident in her ashen skin and the tick at the corner of one dry red-rimmed eye.

"Dad didn't post your bail. He still believes you're guilty." A pause. "Everyone does."

Disappointment filled him as she emphasized *everyone*. "Then why are you here?"

"The detectives have more questions for me." She dodged his gaze. "I don't know how much more I can tell them. I didn't put through any payments. You did."

"Damn it, Gina, you know me!" Asher tempered his tone when she flinched, and finished, "How can you think I had anything to do with it?"

"What else am I to think?" Her eyes flashed. "You authorized all the financial transactions that went missing."

"I didn't make those payments. I swear everything I did was legitimate."

"Obviously not, or the money wouldn't have vanished." She paused for a second, before adding with low vehemence, "Can't you just admit what you did and take responsibility?"

Asher recalled how the public defender had presented what would happen if he admitted what he'd done and returned the money or kept pleading his innocence and took his chances in court. Guilty or not, he was screwed.

"I'm not going to admit to something I didn't do."

Gina's expression closed down. Her next words demonstrated that she didn't have the tiniest amount of sympathy for him. "You don't seem to realize that the entire family is suffering because of what happened with the festival. Our family name is ruined. And there's talk that we could be kicked out of the Cattleman's Club because of this."

Her words gutted him. Asher stood rooted to the spot as she dodged around him and headed toward the reception desk. In a daze, he made for the exit, forgetting that he was no longer free to move around at will until he reached the sidewalk and became aware of the electronic monitor's unfamiliar weight rubbing against his ankle.

He was on house arrest until his trial. Whenever that was. While this situation was better than being stuck in jail, he still chaffed at the restrictions. Of course, he could venture out in Lani's company. As long as she notified the officials of their movements, he could accompany her on excursions. He had only to persuade her he could help her investigation.

Bolstered by determination, Asher glanced around, unsure how he was supposed to get back to Elegance Ranch to begin his court-ordered confinement. No doubt his car remained at The Edmond Organization. He doubted anyone had thought to remove it from the parking lot. Should he head there to pick it up? How much trouble would he be in if he didn't go straight home?

Asher started to pull his phone out of his pocket only to remember that it had been seized as evidence. How was he supposed to arrange a ride home without it? He could probably go inside and borrow a phone to call someone, but then remembered how Gina had acted toward him. What if everyone said no? He was a pariah now. No one would want to touch him with a ten-foot pole.

Cursing under his breath, he stood on the sidewalk and struggled to recall a moment when he'd felt more helpless. He'd been in plenty of dicey situations where he'd survived thanks to skill and/or good luck. His current predicament was unique and terrifying because he had no clue how to fix what was happening to him.

He couldn't run or charm his way out of the situation. This was a problem he had to face head-on. Usually when disquieting emotions erupted, he'd turn his attention to something pleasant. Naturally Lani's image popped into his head, and as he recalled their conversation earlier that day, the frantic thrumming of his nerves eased.

Almost as if his powerful need had summoned her, a black SUV pulled up to the curb and the passenger-side window rolled down. The woman behind the wheel turned her head in his direction. Her eyes, hidden behind aviator sunglasses, Lani regarded him for a heartbeat, assessing him. A moment later, she issued a two-word command.

"Get in."

Asher didn't hesitate. He needed help and Lani had appeared as if in answer to his prayer. Grinning at this uptick in his fortune, he opened the door and got in.

"Thanks for—"

"Save it."

Her grim expression declared just how untrustworthy he'd become in her eyes. Yet for some reason this didn't set him back the way it should. As dark as things had become in the last few days, Lani was here. She'd come to his rescue. No matter what she said, deep down, some part of her believed he wasn't capable of stealing millions of dollars.

"How did you know I was out of jail?"

"Because I'm the one who paid your bail. I need access to you in order to do my job and that's impossible with you behind bars."

Not the rousing endorsement of his innocence he was hoping for, but he was thrilled to have her on his team even if his freedom was nothing more than a means to an end for her.

"Thanks," he repeated. Not wanting to irritate her further, he quelled the urge to say more.

She took her foot off the brake and the car rolled forward. Lani drove with the same focus she applied to everything. As if by sheer force of will, she could control what happened next. Yet Asher perceived several hairline cracks in her confidence. His former lover gripped the steering wheel like it was the gunnel of a pitching boat while her attention remained locked on the road ahead of them as if expecting sinkholes to open up out of nowhere.

"My car is at The Edmond Organization," he said, noticing that she was headed in the opposite direction. "If you want to drop me off."

"It's not there."

"What do you mean it's not there?"

"Your car has been seized by investigators. They are going over it now."

Asher's skin prickled. "Why?"

"They're looking for evidence."

"In my car?" he demanded.

"Your car. Your devices. Your home and office."

As if spending the night in jail and being shunned by his family hadn't been stressful enough, it appeared as if nothing in his life was going to escape unscathed by this mess.

He squashed his disappointment and lapsed into resigned silence as they headed out of town in the direction of Elegance Ranch, the Edmond family estate. The thought of being stuck in his apartment over the barn for the uncertain future gave Asher the chills. He hated being tied down... It was part of the reason his job at Edmond Oil frustrated him. There was no thrill or exhilaration being tied to a desk.

And that was why he'd jumped at the chance to be involved with the festival. It was a much-needed break from his routine. If only the whole thing hadn't failed so spectacularly. Maybe it would've turned out if he'd kept a better eye on everything. Not that he could've predicted the tornado that destroyed the place. But if he'd paid more attention to what was going on, maybe he wouldn't have been caught flat-footed with millions of dollars missing and all signs pointing straight at him like a ring of laser sights aimed at his head and heart.

"I want to hire you," Asher declared abruptly, turning his head to stare at her elegant profile. "To prove I'm innocent," he clarified, determined to do or say whatever it took to get her on his side.

"I already have a client."

He refused to be deterred. "You can work for both of us at the same time."

"You can't afford me," she reminded him with a hint of a smirk. "Your assets are frozen."

"I have ways of generating cash."

Her dark eyebrows rose above her sunglasses. "You've found someone else to steal from?"

He ignored the flippant jab. "I have twelve horses I'm training as polo mounts. They aren't all ready to go, but selling a couple of them would pay your fees."

Lani shook her head. "It's not just about the money. It would be a conflict of interest to work for you while I've been hired to investigate the theft and find the money."

"The way I see it, he hired you to get to the truth." Asher kept a close eye on her reaction to his reasoning. "I know I didn't steal the money. So, if I hire you for the same reason, then you don't have to be worried about any conflicts of interest."

She rolled her gaze his direction before returning her attention to the highway. "My intention is to find out what's going on. I'm not going to stop until I get to the bottom of what happened to the money."

"Good. Then we're on the same side."

"We're *not*." His assumption had obviously set a spark to her temper. "Just to be completely clear, I believe you had the means and the opportunity to steal that money. I'm really good at what I do. I will find out what happened and where the money went. And when I do, I'll know who's guilty and who's not."

Asher pressed his point. "That's fine with me because I swear to you that I didn't take the money."

"Gaslighting won't work on me." She paused and took in his confused expression. "Gaslighting. Where you keep saying something over and over in the hopes that I'll eventually believe that it's reality."

"If I'm repeating the same thing over and over, it's because I'm telling the truth."

"Let's just agree to disagree," she said, echoing something he'd said to her before they parted ways five years earlier.

It hadn't been the words as much as his dismissive tone as he'd delivered the cliché. Afterward she spent a lot of time thinking about how that abrupt breakup made her feel. What bothered her at the time was how he hadn't taken her concerns seriously. She'd not felt heard. Her feelings had been swept aside as if they hadn't matter. As if *she* hadn't mattered to him.

And that, in a nutshell, was what had been wrong with their relationship the whole time. It hadn't just been a summer fling for her. She hadn't had enough experience with men to be able to lock her heart in a box and engage in some truly phenomenal sex as if it were some sort of trendy new aerobic exercise.

Maybe if he hadn't been her first, she would've been more emotionally sophisticated. More capable of keeping their relationship in perspective. Of realizing that no matter how special he treated her in an effort to get her into bed, it was all just a means to an end. She'd been little more than a distraction that summer, a fact that had become clear when he'd never contacted her again.

Neither one of them spoke until Asher gave her the key code to unlock the gate.

"Are you still in the apartment above the stables?" she asked, angling toward the driveway that led past the main house.

"I prefer the horses to Rusty's company."

Lani shored up her resolve as a smile ghosted across

his lips. The last thing she needed was to get sucked in by Asher's attempt to manipulate her emotions. He needed her on his side, a friendly ear to fill with his tales of woe. Well, she wasn't going to fall for his tactics. She wasn't on his side. And nothing he said or did was going to change that.

She parked the SUV behind the stables and while Asher slid out of the vehicle, Lani reached for the duffel bag she'd stashed in the back. He glanced at it as she joined him at the base of the stairs that led to the two-bedroom apartment above the barn.

"What's in the bag?"

A little tingle of excitement danced across her skin. "I'm planning on staying here while I get to the bottom of what's going on."

"Staying here?" he echoed, his expression softening with interest. "With *me*?"

Oh, no. She recognized that look. Her pulse jumped at the implications. Whatever assumptions he was making, she needed to shut him down ASAP.

"This isn't a booty call," she declared, wincing at her raspy tone. "You have two bedrooms. I'm planning on using the one you don't sleep in."

"You're welcome to, of course," he murmured, watching her from beneath heavy lids, a smoky glow kindling in his gaze. "But are you sure you'll be comfortable alone here with me?"

Oh, she'd definitely be uncomfortable sharing four walls with him, but with the future of her business riding on this investigation, she intended to keep things professional between her and Asher.

Don't worry about my comfort, frat boy. Worry about

the mountain of evidence against you. It's what she should've shot back. But that's not what came out.

"I have no intention of sleeping with you ever again." Even as the declaration escaped her, Lani knew she'd overreacted.

"Okay." He drew the word out while peering at her expression. "It seems to me that you had no intention of sleeping with me five years ago, but look how great that turned out."

Lani noted the heat surging through her veins at his smugness and registered annoyance and impatience. Not desire. Not yearning. She was angry at him for reminding her of something she couldn't forget.

"I didn't know what I was doing back then."

"Maybe not at first," he agreed, misinterpreting her response. While she sputtered in mortified dismay, one side of his mouth kicked up into a wicked grin. "But you sure got the hang of things. And if I remember correctly, you even managed to teach me a thing or two."

Cheeks flaming, Lani silently cursed. From the moment she'd agreed to take this gig, she'd warned herself to remain focused on the case and not rehash how their summer romance had played out.

"Why don't we concentrate on the present," she suggested in a desperate rush, once again questioning her wisdom in taking on this assignment.

He gave a lazy one-shoulder shrug. "You're the one bringing up our past."

She set her foot onto the stairs and stomped up the stairs ahead of him. Why hadn't she argued more vigorously against Kingston Blue's insistence that she was a perfect investigator to take on the mystery of the missing millions? Every time she tried to follow her instincts when it came to this man, the best way forward was always murky.

Reaching the landing at the top, she shifted to one side and waited for Asher to enter the unlock code, but he merely turned the knob and pushed open the door.

"After you," he gestured with exaggerated gallantry.

Lani stared at the door. "You don't lock it?"

"What's the point? There's fencing all around the property and a gate at the entrance. Who should I worry about getting inside? Ross? Gina? Rusty?"

"They're not the only people who live here. What about Ross's college friend?"

"Billy Holmes?" Asher chuckled. "The guesthouse where he's staying is way nicer than this. Besides, he doesn't seem the type to show up uninvited."

"But there are parties on the property. And staff. How many people have access to your apartment?"

"I never thought about it." He made a shooing gesture to urge her inside. "And anyway, I don't keep anything of value for someone to steal."

"That watch you're wearing isn't cheap."

He glanced down at the Breitling on his wrist and from his surprised expression, he obviously didn't register the ten-thousand-dollar accessory as being anything out of the ordinary. Lani didn't know whether to laugh or hit him. Five years ago, dating him had opened up a whole new world for her. She'd grown up in a comfortable middle-class home and never lacked for anything, but once she'd been drawn into Asher's circle, she'd gotten a firsthand glimpse into all the finest things money could buy.

Not that this had anything to do with why she'd gone out with him that first time. In fact his determination to buy her affection with huge tips had reinforced her resistance to his pursuit. Still, dating him had swept her into a fairy tale and she'd enjoyed being a princess for a little while.

"Holy sh—"

Asher's shock roused Lani from her musings. The apartment was torn apart—every cabinet in the kitchen was open, plates, cups, pans and silverware all over the countertops and floor. The couch cushions had been pulled apart and the small desk near one of the windows had been ransacked.

"What did they think I was hiding?"

His shoulders sagged as he rubbed his face. Sympathy whiplashed through Lani before she could steel herself against it. To her dismay, the profound defeat gripping Asher did little to distract from his sex appeal. In fact she was seized by an overwhelming urge to slide her arms around his broad shoulders and revisit the intense physical connection she'd only known with one man. *This* man.

Lani ground her teeth and slapped some sense into her emotions. She might no longer be in love with him, but his ability to burrow beneath her skin was alive and well.

"This is definitely worse than I expected," she murmured, bemused by the devastation. "Why don't you go grab a shower while I clean up."

After tossing her duffel bag into the empty bedroom, Lani put in earbuds and set to work putting the kitchen back together. Given that the theft had happened electronically, they could've been looking for a thumb drive and something that small could be anywhere. She swept scattered pasta and cereal into the trash and loaded the dishes and drinkware back into the cabinets. Sorting the silverware into the drawers took some time and as she worked, Lani couldn't help but wonder if the investigators had left the mess as a warning to Asher or if they'd had a limited amount of time to complete a thorough search.

She didn't notice Asher had returned until a light tap on her shoulder caused her to whirl around. He was standing right there, inches away, smelling of soap and minty toothpaste. Her brain went off-kilter as she stared at his lips, moving as they formed words she couldn't hear because…

He plucked her left earbud free and before she could make a grab for it, he'd fitted it into his ear. One eyebrow shot up as he listened to the song.

"I thought you only listened to Lowercase when you were worried about something."

His question was the yummy center of a raspberry-filled donut. Her mouth watered as if the sugary-sweetness flowed across her taste buds. How was it possible that he'd remembered her obscure taste in music after all this time?

"It helps me think." Lowercase was a music genre built around unheard ambient sounds.

"What are you thinking about?"

Lani held her hand out for the earbud, not wanting him to read anything into tonight's musical choice. His fingertips grazed her palm as he dropped the one he'd taken back into her keeping. Weathering the zing of pleasure at the contact, she popped both earbuds back into their case and slid it into her jacket pocket.

"This case. My next steps."

"You always have a plan, don't you?" He sounded resigned.

"It beats running around without direction, hoping something will develop."

"If you plan for everything, nothing will surprise you." He spun her around and tugged the elastic band down her ponytail, freeing her long hair. "I've really missed this," he murmured, threading his fingers through the dark curtain, fanning it over her shoulders. Several strands spilled over her cheeks, tickling her skin. "Your hair is like satin. I've never known anything like it."

She stood transfixed as he gathered her hair together and then proceeded to separate the strands into three sections. The gentle pull as he began braiding launched her into the past. The first time he'd done this for her she'd been surprised by his skill. He'd explained that while a polo horse's mane was shaved to keep it from interfering with the reins, the tails were braided and taped up for competition.

"There you go," he murmured, securing the bottom of the braid and giving an affectionate little tug the way he always did. "Ready for bed."

With her skin awash in goose bumps, Lani turned to face him. They were standing so close. As he leaned into her space, she gathered soft folds of his T-shirt, clutching the material between trembling fingers, needing something to ground her.

Cupping the back of her neck, he lowered his forehead until it was touching hers. "Thank you."

These weren't the words she'd been expecting him to say and frustration spiked.

"Asher." His name whispered out of her in protest, in longing. "Please stop thanking me."

"I can't," he murmured. "You're the only one who's helping me."

"I'm on a case. That's all there is to it." Yet even as she restated her purpose, her spine arched ever so slightly to bring her torso into contact with his. After an instant of contact, her breasts grazing his chest, she retreated.

This was madness. She had to stop this. To back away. But with his breath caressing her heated skin, she couldn't move. All it would take for their lips to come together was the slightest shift from either of them.

Temptation gnawed at her common sense. Her whole body ached with longing. She hadn't been celibate in the years since they'd parted, but no man awakened her hunger like Asher. It wasn't fair that his body could drive her wild with pleasure when his temperament clashed with everything she believed in.

Tingles shot down her spine as the tips of his fingers caressed her nape, moved along the side of her neck. Lani nerves sang. Desire moved through her like a ghost, terrifying her. How long had they been standing here like this? Seconds? Minutes? Time blurred when Asher touched her.

Kissing him would set a bad precedent. Her professionalism was a press of lips away from being thrown out the window. On the other hand, her job was to find the festival funds. A kiss hinted that her belief in his guilt was fading. Pretending to be on his side could convince him to trust her. What happened after she figured out where Asher had hidden the money was a problem for the future.

"Lani." The low throb in his voice intensified the ache blooming between her thighs.

"Yes?"

As he grazed his knuckles along her jaw, her lips parted in anticipation and her breath rushed out in agitated puffs as every nerve in her body went on full alert. He set his thumb beneath her chin, a promise of what came next. Craving a barely-there brush of her lips against his, she rose on tiptoe just the tiniest bit. She'd lost control of her purpose. But instead of a kiss that curled her toes and inspired her to dance in the moonlight, he planted his lips against her forehead.

"See you in the morning."

Lani reeled back a step and cleared her throat, blathering out the first thing that popped into her mind. "Sure. I'll be here when you get up."

"Sleep well."

Before he walked away, his dark eyes searched hers, and a small perceptive smile tugged at the corners of his lips. If her skin weren't already on fire, she was certain she'd be flushing scarlet beneath his knowing look. She'd thought to play him and instead he'd expertly turned the tables on her. Lani sighed. She'd been a fool to suppose a single kiss would propel Ash to confess his guilt and spill his guts. She was playing with fire letting the old chemistry between them ignite once more.

Yet the tactic could still work if she could manage to act the part without getting sucked in.

Five years ago she'd been slow to trust Asher, but eventually his persistence and irresistible sex appeal had worn her down. Once her hormones had seized the wheel, they'd driven her heart straight into a solid brick wall of misery.

This time, while she might be too wise to tumble head over heels for his effortless charm and handsome face, if she kept missing signs and misinterpreting signals, she could be in way too deep before she knew what hit her.

Despite not having slept at all in the jail cell the night before, Asher lay in the middle of his king-size bed, hands tucked beneath his head, ankles crossed, eyes tracing shadows on the ceiling. He'd retreated to his bedroom a couple hours ago, but adrenaline still surged through his veins, keeping him awake.

Lani Li was here. In his home. Sleeping ten strides from where he lay. The thrill of it kept his exhaustion at bay. He pictured her curled on her side, long braid coiled around her throat, her thick straight lashes a dark smudge against her ivory cheeks.

Not one thing about her had changed in the last five years. She continued to be the most intense, uptight, no-nonsense female he'd ever met. Except in bed where uptight and no-nonsense had given away to curious and naughty.

He'd been her first. The shock that delivered to his system had cemented her as the most memorable woman he'd ever had in his bed.

His lips still tingled from the silken heat of her skin when he'd kissed her forehead. They'd both been on the verge of moving too fast, of losing themselves in the fierce chemistry between them. Last time she'd been an innocent and he'd won her by awakening her sensual appetites. And then he'd lost her because he'd failed to treat her heart with the same care.

Asher hadn't realized how much he'd missed her until she'd appeared in front of his jail cell. Probably because after they'd ended things, he'd gone out of his way to purge her from his system.

With his thoughts filled with Lani, he finally fell asleep and woke with her foremost in his mind late the next morning. From the position of the light, he could tell it was mid to late morning. Reaching toward the nightstand for his phone, he remembered the police still had it. Cursing, he sat up and noticed the scent of coffee mingling with bacon. His stomach growled, reminding him that he'd skipped dinner the night before.

Pulling on worn jeans and a black polo shirt, he shuffled into the open-concept kitchen and living room and spied Lani at the kitchen island, typing away on her laptop.

"You made breakfast," he murmured unnecessarily, checking out the pan on the stove. "Have you already eaten?"

She didn't look up from her computer. "Hours ago."

"I didn't sleep at all the night before." He clamped down on further excuses and poured a cup of coffee, topping hers off in the process. After doctoring his cup, he pushed the sugar and creamer in her direction.

The eggs were freshly cooked and exactly as he

liked them. His heart bumped against his ribs as he surveyed the scrambled eggs with fried onions and cheddar cheese melted through. He finished them off in record time and stood watching her work, gnawing on the final piece of thick-cut bacon.

"Stop staring at me," Lani muttered, picking up the coffee cup near her elbow and sipping the strong brew.

"Why?" He ran hot water over the pan and dishes before sliding them into the dishwasher. "You're the most interesting thing around."

"You can stop right there. I'm not susceptible to flattery."

"The fact that you felt the need to tell me that makes me think otherwise." He sent his gaze trailing over her features. She was even more beautiful than she'd been five years earlier. "And I'm not trying to flatter you. It's the truth. You fascinated me from the moment I first laid eyes on you."

"Don't confuse what happened between us five years ago to what's going on between us today. You are a *job*. Nothing more. I bailed you out because I need you to tell me where you stashed the money."

He was pondering how long she would stick around before his inability to provide the information she needed would cause her to give up on him…again… when she let out an impatient huff.

"Shouldn't you be doing something productive right now?" She jerked her head, indicating the apartment's front door.

He had horses he could exercise, but they would keep for a little while longer.

"I thought you needed my help with your case."

"Not right this second."

Coming around to her side of the island, he leaned his forearm on the cool countertop and peered at her laptop screen. Their shoulders bumped and he hid a grin as she shifted away. Obviously his presence bothered her. He could work with that.

"You are always so single-minded. At first, I thought that was just a cute personality quirk until I got to know you better. Then I realized how incredibly sexy your intense focus could be."

He'd barely finished speaking when she slapped the laptop closed and slid off the barstool.

"To be clear," she said, sliding the computer into a protective sleeve, "I am not here because I have any interest in starting up anything with you again. Let's just keep things between us professional."

"I don't see why I should have to do that. It's not as if I'm a client or anything."

"I'm investigating you," she reminded him.

"You're looking for the missing festival funds and trying to discover the real story. That puts us on the same side. Nothing wrong with hooking up with a fellow truth-seeker, is there?"

"Hooking up...?" Outrage crackled in her voice. "Don't even get me started on how wrong it is."

"You used to find me irresistible."

"You had your moments." She slipped into the same blazer she'd worn the day before and slung a tote bag over her shoulder, signaling her plans to leave. "Your situation was completely different back then."

Meaning that he might have been a *frat boy* but, as far as she knew, he hadn't been a criminal. Was his appearance of guilt all that stood between them? Would she relent once it became clear he hadn't stolen any money? Or should he get her back into his bed so she'd be motivated to clear him? Either way he would win. Cleared of all wrongdoing and Lani as his lover once more.

The whole thing seemed so simple until he remembered the strong evidence mounted against him. Just because he hadn't stolen from the festival, didn't mean he wouldn't go to jail for the theft. So far, his denials hadn't convinced anyone of his innocence. Nor should he expect to be taken at his word. Buying that damning house in his name in the Maldives had been clever. Somebody was setting him up. But who? Was it possible that someone had stolen his identity? He recalled Lani's reaction to his unlocked door. Maybe it wasn't far-fetched. But how did he go about proving something like that? No doubt she had the resources to follow the money. But how did he steer her to look for whoever had framed him when she was so convinced he was the bad guy?

"Where are you off to?" he asked.

"I have to meet a new client."

Asher loathed the idea of being left all alone with his problems. "Can I come along?" Even as he offered her his most-winning smile, he felt like a puppy begging to go for a car ride.

"No."

He strode into the kitchen and selected the largest knife in the drawer. Lani watched him through narrowed eyes as he set his foot on the counter and slid his finger beneath the strap that kept the electronic monitor on his ankle.

"What do you think you're doing?" Lani's voice rang with annoyance.

"I suffer from separation anxiety," he declared, carrying the dog metaphor beyond the absurd. "There's no telling what I'll get up to if you leave me alone here."

"Don't be ridiculous," she snapped, but her eyes remained glued to the knife. "You are perfectly fine on your own."

"Normally." He tested the edge of the blade with his thumb. A line of red appeared. Damn, it was sharper than he'd expected. "But I'm under a great deal of stress at the moment and I might do something completely rash without someone to keep an eye on me. Like maybe remove this monitor." He paused. "How much is my bail?"

"A hundred thousand." She ground out the number between clenched teeth.

"That's a lot. And you're responsible for me, right?"

Her nostrils flared as she sucked in a sharp breath. "Asher."

"Let me come along and I swear I won't be any trouble."

"Your middle name is trouble," she muttered. "Fine. I'll call and let the people monitoring you know that we're heading to Dallas."

"I'll put on some shoes."

Ten minutes later they were speeding toward Dallas with Lani behind the wheel and Asher studying her profile. She was trying to appear impassive, but her tight lips betrayed her inner turmoil.

"So, how come you're a private investigator?" he said, breaking the stony silence between them. "What happened to becoming a fed?"

"I got in." Her knuckles turned white as she clutched the steering wheel. "But in the course of my training, the amount of gender discrimination I encountered was more than I could stand. The good ol' boy network is alive and well at the FBI. Eighty percent of the trainees discharged prior to graduation are women and that's mostly because the people in charge dismiss mistakes made by male trainees as isolated incidents and declare them to be retrainable at a disproportionately higher rate than their female trainee counterparts."

"I'm sorry," he murmured, hearing the pain she was trying to mask with a clinical recitation of facts. "I know that was important to you."

So important that she'd chosen to pursue the dream over him.

"Tell me more about your firm,"

"I started it two years ago after finishing up with my master's degree. I worked with an investigator for a year before striking out on my own."

"You must be doing pretty well."

A shadow passed over her face before she mustered an off-handed shrug. "I'm doing okay."

But not as well as she'd like to be doing. Asher tapped his fingers on his thigh. His restless nature intensified when he was stressed or bored. Usually being around Lani calmed him, but he'd picked up on her tension and found himself uneasily pondering why she hadn't pursued law enforcement the way she'd intended.

"What sort of investigations do you do?"

"I've made a name for myself as a financial investigator. Divorces. Fraud. Embezzlement." Her gaze twitched his direction at the last word.

"You carry a gun," Asher pointed out. "Is there a lot of violence in financial investigations? I would've figured it would be done by being in an enclosed room with a computer."

"I do what needs to be done. I have a technical guy that does contract work for me, a cyber specialist who can get all sorts of information."

"Legally?"

A muscle jumped in her jaw. "If you're asking whether he can dig into everything you do online, then the answer is yes. There aren't too many secrets that escape Donovan."

"So, he's looking into me." He paused, giving her room to answer, but when she remained silent, he continued, "When you find out that I'm an open book with no secrets at all, will you trust me then?"

"*Trust* is a word I don't use lightly when it comes to you."

"But if you don't find anything," he persisted, "you'll have to believe me when I tell you I had nothing to do with the missing money."

"Or you're just real clever."

Asher gave a wry snort. "Well, at long last I have something to crow about. Lani Li just called me clever."

She shot him a look. "You make it sound like I think you're stupid. That's never been the case. What I think you are is underachieving."

He winced at her blunt, if mostly accurate, declaration. As a teenager, when he'd failed to win his adoptive father's approval, frustration had led to resentment. The things Asher had a passion for, activities he excelled at—polo, extreme sports, playing the stock market—were never going to impress Rusty.

Yet deep down he still clung to the hope that one day the impossible old man would be proud of his adopted son. It was part of what had prompted Asher to switch gears and take a job he hated with The Edmond Organization. But as the months went by and Rusty was as indifferent as ever, Asher realized he'd made a mistake.

Maybe if his dad had lived and Asher could've had a father who loved him unconditionally, he might have had a solid foundation to build something out of his life. Often he'd wished for a positive paternal figure who'd listen to him and offered advice based on what he enjoyed doing. Instead, Rusty had ignored or criticized him in turns. With support, he might've been able to focus on what he loved. To fully commit instead of fighting against other people's expectations and always falling short.

"You're right about that," Asher said, not letting his angst slip into his tone. "Ask anyone in the family. I'm the quintessential underachiever."

"You don't seem thrilled to be working at The Edmond Organization," she said. "So, why are you doing it?"

"Rusty got tired of supporting me and decided to give me the choice of working for the company or being cut off." At least that's what everyone assumed was going on because that was part of the bargain he'd made with Rusty.

"Let me get this straight." She took her eyes off the

road and speared him with a dubious look. "You gave up polo and came to work for the company in order to keep your lifestyle intact?"

"Seems like the obvious choice, don't you think?"

She didn't react to his flippant tone. "Obvious, maybe, but you don't seem happy."

"Since when are you an expert on what makes me happy?" he shot back, still pained by her blunt opinion of him all those years earlier.

What made the sting so much sharper is that she hadn't been wrong. He'd loved playing polo, but he hadn't played up to his abilities. He hadn't had to with Rusty's money backing him.

"I'm not," she said, her voice somewhat softening with regret. "I'm sorry I said that. I don't know you at all and have no business making assumptions."

"No, I'm sorry." He rubbed his chest where a tight knot had formed. Damn. "It's just that I never imagined our reunion happening because I was accused of embezzlement and that you'd believe I was guilty."

"Wait." She frowned in confusion. "You imagined that we'd have a reunion?"

"Sure."

"Unbelievable," she muttered, tossing an indignant look his way. "Then why haven't I heard from you in five years?"

Three

Lani breathed slowly in and out through her nose, struggling against the anguish that had just blindsided her. Damn it. Why had she asked that ridiculous question? Now the infuriating man would think it bothered her that they'd never reconnected.

"I don't have a good answer," Asher admitted, sounding more subdued than he had a moment earlier.

"Of course you don't."

Why couldn't she stop being surprised when he disappointed her? After all, she'd traveled to Royal to investigate him for embezzling millions of dollars.

"Did you want me to?"

"I…" Had she?

Lani's heart began to race. Once upon a time she'd prided herself on being straightforward and honest with people. Experience had taught her that this tactic didn't always produce the results she desired. Bottom line? She learned to mislead people in her pursuit of the truth or justice for her clients.

Kingston Blue had chosen her because of her past romantic connection with Asher. Was it wrong to take advantage of that to get him to trust her? If she appeared to believe he was innocent, maybe he'd drop his defenses and slip up.

"Well?" he prompted.

"It would've been nice to hear from you," she admitted, keeping her tone from revealing her inner conflict.

"Really?" He practically vibrated with curiosity. "The way things ended, I thought you'd be happy never to hear from me again."

"Yes...well." She couldn't give in immediately or he'd be suspicious. He had to work for it.

"You were pretty mad the last time we talked," he reminded her.

"You told me a long-distance thing between us would never work after I told you I thought I was falling in love you, and then when I asked how you felt about me, you said you liked me, but didn't think it was that serious between us." Acutely aware of Asher's gaze on her, Lani stared straight ahead and resisted the urge to glance his way. She focused on calm thoughts to reduce the heat scorching her cheeks as she revisited the humiliating scene. "And then you said it wasn't your intention to upset me."

"See, I was right. You are still mad at me."

"For pulling that typical guy crap and turning the whole disagreement back on me? You bet I am!" Her temper flared. "As if I was being unreasonable because I wanted to keep things going."

"Even though it would never have worked?"

Lani released a frustrated breath. "We could've at least tried." But agreeing to attempt a long-distance relationship would mean he had feelings for her and that had obviously not been the case.

"What can I do to make it up to you?"

He could tell her where the money went. "Not a damned thing."

"I don't believe that."

"Really. I don't want you to make anything up to me. We went our separate ways five years ago and it was for the best. In fact, I should thank you. Dragging things out in an effort to make it work and then failing would've been a lot harder in the end."

"Lani..."

She gave her head a vigorous shake to keep him from saying something that would make her wonder... was there a way they could find their way to each other this time?

"Let's just keep the past where it belongs and focus on keeping things professional between us."

To her relief, Asher lapsed into silence and focused his attention on the landscape speeding past them. Lani let out an inaudible sigh.

Why was she surprised to be no closer to figuring out what made him tick than she had been all those years ago? Back then, little had seemed to bother him. The only thing that seemed to get under his skin was the way his adoptive father treated him with such indifference and even when she'd asked him about it, Asher had shrugged it off as Rusty's issue, not his.

Asher was an expert at putting up a good front, never admitting anything was wrong, never asking for help. His reluctance to dwell on anything that made him uncomfortable had made it hard for them to develop the sort of intimate connection Lani craved. Not that this stopped her from falling deeper under his spell with each day that passed. And yet, despite his unwillingness to share how his father's death had affected him, she sensed that the loss left him unsure how to let people in.

Maybe if he'd opened up to her, shown that he needed her, she might not have given up on him so easily. But she couldn't figure out where she fit in his life and in the end she'd let him go.

Which had relieved her parents to no end. They'd been afraid she'd put off her education to run around the world with some rich, entitled polo player, thus ruining her life. While staying on the path she'd laid out for herself had been sensible, her decision wasn't without regret. Especially after her dreams of a career in the FBI had abruptly ended. Add in her struggles to build her business, and she sometimes wondered if she could've been happy following Asher from Argentina to England and all over the US.

One thing was for sure, she never imagined he'd take a position at the family organization. She knew he must have hated being tied down and yet didn't Rusty's threat to cut him off if he quit feed perfectly into a motive for Asher to steal the money? The amount that had gone missing would've funded his polo playing for many years. Or had he planned to roam the globe in search of thrilling adventures?

Yet Asher made it sound like he was relying on the Edmond family fortune when she'd noticed that he'd moved up the ranks and started doing really well as a professional polo player. His Twitter feed reflected numerous endorsements and photo shoots he'd done, capitalizing on his good looks. He'd engaged in a fair amount of philanthropic work, as well. So why was he promoting the impression that he'd been barely getting by without Rusty's money?

"Tell me something about the client you're meeting," Asher prompted, pulling Lani from her thoughts.

For a moment she thought of refusing, but talking about her work beat brooding over this man. "She came to me because her husband is cheating on her and she wants to make sure she has a clear financial picture to take to her divorce lawyer."

"I don't know why men do that."

"Do what?" she quizzed, shooting a sidelong glance his way. "Get married, cheat or hide money?"

"Get married and then cheat." Was he thinking about Rusty who'd been married four times—once for three years to Asher's mother—and was currently single and definitely mingling? "What's the point of agreeing to love someone 'til death do you part only to change your mind a few years later?"

"Is that why you never got married?" she found herself asking.

"I never got married because playing professional polo kept me from settling down with the right woman."

Was he talking in generalities or had his heart been

claimed before or since they'd been together? The question raised all the insecurities she'd experienced that summer. The vividness of her reaction was like standing next to a warning siren when it went off. Her muscles twitched in response, sending a pulse of adrenaline through her.

"You seem to have settled down now, so why haven't you reached out?"

"Who says I haven't?"

"Is she in a relationship or married?"

"Neither. But she doesn't really trust that I'm not the same man she once knew."

Lani wasn't sure how to answer him. Nor could she figure out why she was pouring lemon juice on an old cut that had never fully healed. At least she knew why he hadn't wanted to try a long-distance relationship with her. Obviously he'd never gotten over the woman he'd once loved.

"You should get in touch with her. She might surprise you."

"She might," Asher murmured, his expression pensive.

With the mood between them growing incredibly awkward, Lani was thrilled that her office was only five minutes away. She pulled into the underground parking garage and slipped into her dedicated spot. Now that she and Asher had arrived, Lani was quite sure that agreeing to let him tag along had been the wrong decision.

"There's a café and lounge on the first floor where you can wait," she said, snagging her laptop out of the back seat and slipping from the SUV. "My meeting shouldn't take too long."

"Do you mind if I come along? I'd like to see your office."

"It would be better if you didn't."

Asher pointed to his ankle monitor. "Separation anxiety, remember?"

Since Lani couldn't trust him to refrain from doing something that might blow back on her, she had no choice but to agree. And she couldn't ignore that she wanted to show off a little. The spot she'd chosen for her firm was north of downtown Dallas in a glass-enclosed building with great views. Her office was on the eighth floor. She shared a spacious waiting area with a lawyer and an accountant and had done work for both of them in the year since she'd moved in.

"This is me," she declared unnecessarily a few minutes later, unlocking the door to the dual-office suite and making her way down the hall.

Entering her airy workspace with its glass walls and north-facing windows, she circled her desk and woke up her computer to check if any email had come in during the drive from Royal.

Asher glanced around the space, noting the light spilling in the floor-to-ceiling windows. The room was spacious enough to accommodate a table with four chairs, her desk and a pair of guest chairs.

"Who works there?"

Lani looked up. His attention had shifted toward the empty workspace they'd passed. "No one at the moment." Seeing his curiosity hadn't been satisfied, she sighed. "When I leased the space, I'd hoped to expand. Add an associate. I still plan to. It's just that I don't have enough business at the moment." Hopefully that would change once she completed this job for Kingston Blue. "So, now that you've seen my office…" She hoped he'd take the hint and leave her to await her client in peace. "Like I said, there's a café downstairs. Or you can sit in the waiting room."

"Why not there?" He indicated the empty office. "No one's using it."

Before Lani could argue, a woman appeared in the open doorway from the waiting room. Shooting Asher a withering glare, Lani smoothed her face and stepped forward to greet the newcomer.

"Hello, I'm Lani Li."

"Mika Sorenson."

Sensing that he'd already pushed his luck too far with Lani, Asher waited until the women were seated before he popped into Lani's office.

"Can I get you anything?" he offered. "Water? Coffee? Soda?" He'd spied a small interior room with a copier, storage and a beverage cooler.

"Nothing for me." Mika gave him an appreciative smile. "Thank you."

"Ms. Li?" The way her eyes flashed, Asher could tell he'd gone too far.

"I'm fine." Her teeth were firmly clenched as she added, "Thank you."

With a smirk Lani's client did not see, Asher ducked out of the room and headed straight into the empty workspace. Because the building was going for a sophisticated modern aesthetic with industrial vibes, glass walls divided this office from the larger one where Lani sat. Asher settled back in the office chair with his back to Lani, and strained to hear the conversation. The women spoke in subdued voices, making it impossible to discern more than a word here or there. Asher had resigned himself to the fact that he wasn't going to learn anything, and was about to head down to the café when a tall man wearing an expensive suit and a stormy expression strode into the office.

When the man's furious gaze locked on Mika Sorenson in Lani's office and his fingers curled into fists, Asher was on his feet and standing in the man's path before the guy had taken more than two steps.

"Can I help you?" Asher demanded in a tone that said he had no intention of being the least bit cooperative.

"That's my wife."

"Okay."

Before Asher could say more, Sorenson's red face contorted in rage and he made as if to charge into Lani's office and take his bad temper out on both women. He set his hand on the man's shoulder, determined to get the guy out of there, but Sorenson was completely focused on his wife.

"You stupid bitch," the man yelled, pushing his weight against Asher in an effort to power past him. "Who the hell do you think you are hiring a private investigator to spy on me?"

The situation was deteriorating fast and Asher had to get the guy out of there. He caught the man's arm in a tight grip. "Let's go."

Although Asher and Sorenson were the same height, the other man lacked Asher's strength. But what Sorenson lacked in muscle, he made up for in outrage.

"Who the hell are you? Let go of me."

"You need to leave," Asher said.

"The hell I do. I'm not going anywhere without my wife."

Asher didn't need to look over his shoulder to know that Mika Sorenson was afraid. And that Lani was not. Years of playing polo had given him the ability to widen his senses and track the ever-changing dynamic of a game where eight players, each riding a thousand-pound horse and swinging a three-foot mallet, all raced after a fist-sized ball. He knew Lani was going to get in the middle of this scuffle and that she might get hurt. Sorenson needed to go before that happened.

"Call security," Asher advised Lani, his gaze never leaving the other man.

Sorenson didn't seem to hear. "Get out of my way."

Keeping his tone mild, Asher responded, "I can't do that."

When the man's fist came toward his face, Asher leaned out of the way. Off balance from the wild swing, Sorenson wasn't at all ready when his opponent snagged his foot and used his own momentum to send him toppling to the floor. Asher winced when Sorenson's head bounced off the hardwood flooring. Convinced Sorenson wasn't about to jump up and go for round two, Asher glanced toward Lani.

Her eyes had gone wide as they bounced from him to the man on the ground. Already adrenaline surged through his veins from the altercation, but seeing the unbridled hunger in Lani's mink-brown gaze, his whole body went up in flames.

"Security," he rasped, wanting nothing more than to take her in his arms and claim the passion parting her soft lips. "You can thank me later." The declaration was both a warning and a promise. Unlike the previous night, there would be no chaste kiss on her forehead. He intended to accept her gratitude in spades.

In the end, with some sense knocked into him, Sorenson left on his own, escorted to the elevator by Asher. When he returned to Lani's office, a white-faced Mika Sorenson was making an appointment with a divorce attorney and Lani was arranging a safe place for her client to temporarily stay.

Lani was standing at her office window, staring out at the storm blowing out of the west when Asher returned from walking Mika to her car in the parking garage. Lightning flashed and the building rumbled as thunder rolled over them. Asher crossed to stand beside her, noting that her tension was as charged as the atmosphere outside.

"Thank you," she muttered, sounding not one bit convincing.

"Oh, you're going to have to do better than that."

She turned toward him, eyes fierce, arms crossed. "Fine. Thank you very much."

Asher snaked his left arm around her waist and brought her up against him hard. "Better," he coaxed, his tone lifting on the latter syllable.

"I don't know what more you want."

"Oh, I think you do." Dragging his knuckles over her flushed cheek, he lowered his head until his lips hung a whisper above hers. "I want you to say it."

"Say what?" The mutinous line of her mouth wavered even as her muscles softened, bringing her pliant curves into sizzling contact with his hard planes.

"Say that you were glad I was here to take care of you and your client today. How having me around was a good thing."

"I could've handled him just fine." She let loose a shocked gasp as he slid his palm up her spine, wrapped his fingers around her ponytail and gave it a sharp tug. "But I'm glad you were here so I didn't have to."

"Better."

The uneven cadence of her breath matched his as he covered her mouth with his in a deep kiss meant to remind her how they'd once burned up the nights. Electricity danced down his spine as his stomach somersaulted. Rain battered the window beside them. And lightning flashed once more, this time behind his eyes as her tongue darted forward to tangle with his. Her sultry moan filled his ears while her warm skin scented the air with roses and jasmine. She lifted her fingertips to his face and ran them over his stubbly cheek. He loved when she touched him like this.

This made sense. Her lips. Kissing her. Feeling once again like some part of him was complete. Why did it only happen when she was in his arms? Everything inside him quieted, making room for this amazing explosion of fulfillment and joy.

Lani angled her head, taking him deeper into her mouth, breathing him in as her fingers tunneled through his hair, nails digging into his scalp. Her lashes were a butterfly kiss against his skin as she pulled him closer, pressing her breasts into his chest and sliding her knee up his thigh as if by wrapping herself around him, they could meld and become one.

Asher lowered his hand to her hip and was seconds

away from cupping her butt and lifting her off her feet when an annoying buzzing sound began. Lani noticed it too and rolled her head back, disengaging from the kiss.

"Ignore it." Issuing the command, he fanned his fingers over her lower back to keep his iron-hard erection firmly pressed into her slowly rocking hips. "Stay just like this," he murmured, in awe of her power over him.

"We shouldn't be…" She twisted free of him, her chest heaving as if she'd finished a mile-long sprint. Scrambling to where her phone was still buzzing madly on her desk, she raked a trembling hand over the tendrils that had escaped her neat ponytail. "Yes?"

Asher leaned back against the cool glass window and shuddered while another boom of thunder rolled through the building. Or was that just the reverberation of his pounding heart? He couldn't catch his breath. The shock of that kiss. Lani's ardent response. How lust had transformed her into living flame… It was all so *exhilarating*. He'd forgotten how intoxicatingly blissful kissing her could be.

He loved her complexities. Straightforward and practical in her role as an investigator and her pursuit of her career goals. Recklessly passionate when it came to her heart. She'd trusted him when she shouldn't have and doubted him when he'd been most honest with her.

While she settled behind the desk and started typing on her keyboard, he let his gaze roam over her lips. She was gnawing on the lower one and he had to look away as sweat prickled his skin.

"Is everything okay?" he asked as she concluded her call.

She'd sat back, narrowed eyes glued to the computer

screen. In the space of ten minutes, she'd cooled to fo-cused professionalism. Meanwhile his defenses were down and his anticipation was sky-high.

"Everything's fine." She did a slow blink and seemed to return from whatever deep dive her brain had done. "Are you ready to go back to Royal?"

"I thought maybe while we're in Dallas we could have dinner." Somewhere romantic and far away from the accusing eyes in Royal so he could lavish his charm on her and see if he could soften her attitude toward him.

She glanced at her phone. "We really need to get back. I already have dinner plans."

"Here in Dallas?" A spike of jealousy caused his voice to harden. Until this moment he hadn't consid-ered that she might be involved with someone. But if she was, would she have kissed him like that?

"No," she said. "In Royal."

"Something having to do with the investigation?" With their passionate embrace sparking his baser in-stincts, Asher was feeling possessive and didn't come off nearly as nonchalant as he'd hoped.

"At the moment the investigation is my main focus."

A non-answer. And from the look on her face, all she was planning to give.

Four

Lani's dinner engagement with Rusty Edmond had stirred a fair amount of interest amongst the members of the Texas Cattleman's Club. Given his family's connection to the Soiree on the Bay debacle, she'd been a little surprised that the oil tycoon wanted to meet in such a public venue. She'd thought he'd prefer to keep a low profile and share a quiet meal somewhere discreet. Instead, as the hostess led her to a table in the middle of the TCC's large dining room, Lani realized that she would be a headliner performing on the center stage.

Great.

It made sense that a man like Rusty Edmond wouldn't be chased away by some negative gossip about his family. No doubt he'd ruffled a lot of feathers while amassing his enormous fortune. What did he care if people whispered about him behind his back?

"Ms. Li." Rusty stood as she approached, his cordial smile not reaching the winter gray of his assessing gaze.

"Mr. Edmond," she countered, wondering if he remembered he'd invited her to call him Rusty the last time they'd met.

The nickname struck her as a blatant attempt to make the man approachable. It was ridiculous. Russell Edmond Sr. was an intimating man by nature. One of the richest oilmen in Texas, he had a mercurial temperament and a roving eye when it came to women.

"Call me Rusty," he rumbled in warm tones, his eyes taking in her measure, lingering a little too long on her breasts for Lani's comfort. Which made her doubly glad she'd resisted the impulse to wear something more flattering. He stuck out his hand as she drew within reach. "May I call you Lani?"

"Of course." As her hand was swallowed in his grip, she was struck by the man's imposing physical presence, as well as the aggressive potency of his personality. "Thank you for agreeing to meet me."

"I understand you bailed my son out of jail."

Okay, so they were diving right in. "I've been hired to investigate where the missing money has gone." *And who took it*.

"Have you asked Asher?" Rusty's expression gave her no clue to whether this was a serious question or if the man was being droll.

"Yes. He claims he didn't steal the money." Lani paused for a beat, waiting for the older man's reaction. "I'm not sure he gains anything by taking it."

Rusty snorted. "He gains millions of dollars."

"Yes, but the theft was so obviously done by him.

Why hadn't he fled before the funds were discovered to be missing? He used part of the money to buy a house in the Maldives. Surely he had to know that would make him the prime suspect."

The waitress stopped by their table and took Lani's drink order. Rusty already had a mostly-empty crystal tumbler sitting in front of him and ordered another whiskey.

"So, you think Asher is innocent." A statement, not a question. "Even though he purchased a house in the Maldives."

"I'm not sure that he did. And he's not the only one with access to the festival accounts who needed money. You disinherited Ross."

Lani paid careful attention to how Rusty reacted to her pointing a finger at his biological son, unsurprised by the man's cold glare. The oil tycoon had cut off Ross several months ago after finding out he'd slept with an employee and fathered a son with her. The tension between Ross and Rusty had eased somewhat in recent weeks, but it was completely possible that Ross might've started skimming the festival funds after such a dramatic reversal in his fortune.

"My son isn't a thief."

Which son? Lani's heart clenched in sympathy for Asher.

"I'm just pointing out that Ross had means, motive and opportunity. And he could've misdirected the investigation so that all the evidence points to Asher."

"Are you trying to say that Asher was set up?"

"It's a possibility."

Skepticism rolled off Rusty. "You two dated a while

back." His lips twisted into disdain. "Are you sure this isn't personal for you?"

Despite preparing to be asked this question, Lani's cheeks heated. The incendiary kiss she and Asher had shared earlier made any denial she might make now a big fat lie.

"I was hired to find the missing money. If the federal investigators believe Asher is guilty, they won't be following any other leads." Lani's gaze clashed with Rusty's wintery one. "If neither Asher nor Ross are guilty, do you have any idea who else might have stolen the funds?"

"I don't." Nor did Rusty Edmond look happy about that. He was a man of decisive action. It must be difficult for him to sit by and let the situation play out. He finished his drink as the waitress set the new tumbler before him and swept away the empty glass. "I recommend the rib eye."

Lani didn't order the eighteen-ounce bone-in steak. Instead she chose a center-cut filet mignon that melted in her mouth. Five years ago Asher had brought her here for dinner. That night she'd been a starry-eyed girl unaccustomed to such lavish service and exquisite cuisine. Watching Rusty attack his own dinner with relish, Lani wondered if any of the Edmond family could survive without their cushy safety net of wealth and privilege.

Although her dinner companion kept turning the conversation away from any further talk of the failed festival or the tornado that had devastated Appaloosa Island the month before, Lani repeatedly circled back. From the way Rusty spoke about Ross, Gina and especially Asher, his pessimistic opinion of them predated any mishandling of Soiree on the Bay. Lani was utterly depressed by the time he waved away the waitress's attempts to list off the daily dessert specials.

She was gathering breath to thank the oil mogul for his time when someone approached their table. Lani recognized Ross's friend Billy Holmes from her preliminary research into everyone connected to the festival. The man's chiseled cheekbones, dark hair and assessing blue eyes combined into a face of arresting handsomeness. Maybe his long nose was a shade too narrow, the cant of his mouth a bit self-indulgent. But as he sized her up in turn, she sensed he knew how to work a room.

Rusty lit up as he and Billy exchanged greetings, startling Lani. She'd heard that Billy had Rusty's ear when his own children couldn't get his attention. Seeing the way the man oozed charm, she understood why Rusty liked him. And apparently so did many of the women. Lani spied four at nearby tables that gazed at Billy with a range of fondness and hunger.

As much as she'd have loved to stick around and ponder this fascinating rapport between the patriarch and his son's good friend, Lani realized her audience with Rusty Edmond had come to an end. Murmuring thanks for the meal, she headed for the exit, eager to share her thoughts with Asher.

But when she arrived back at the ranch, she discovered he wasn't in his apartment. Before panic seized hold, she decided to check the barn. Sure enough, she found him in a grooming stall running a brush over a gray gelding.

"How'd dinner with my father go?" he asked, his voice cool.

Lani winced. She should've known better than to keep quiet about her meeting with Rusty. No doubt her evasiveness had fortified the barriers between them. Maybe subconsciously that had been her plan. Their kiss had shaken her confidence. How could she do her job if emotion disrupted reason? Would she overlook something because she wanted him to be innocent? Worse, what if she found out he was guilty and couldn't bring herself to send him to jail?

"It went okay."

She picked up a brush and went to work on the opposite side of the horse, running the soft bristles over his shoulder and down his front leg.

"Is he the one who hired you to figure out where the money went?" He'd asked the question before and she'd refused to answer. Silence reigned between them for several uncomfortable seconds. "You don't want to talk about it."

"Not really."

As much as Lani wanted to tell Asher that she'd been hired by Kingston Blue, thinking his father had hired her was keeping Asher off balance and she needed whatever advantage she could get if she was going to find the money.

If he was actually responsible for the theft.

While they worked without further conversation, Lani couldn't stop her gaze from chasing the strong lines of Asher's cheekbones and the delectable curve of his lower lip. She shivered as that afternoon's kiss replayed in her mind. The same raw masculinity that had tantalized her five years ago was no less potent, nor had her susceptibility to it dimmed. He'd grown harder in the intervening years. Less indulged rich boy and more a man who wasn't happy with how his life was going.

It's what made him even more interesting. She'd prepared herself to resist his meaningless flirtation and dodge his sexual banter. The melancholy beneath his glib sophistication was more pronounced than ever. He hid it well, but most people probably didn't bother looking past his easy charm and playful humor. She'd trained herself to see into those in-between moments and easily detected the dissatisfaction that plagued him.

"I thought tomorrow I'd head to Appaloosa Island," she said, the idea having come to her on the drive back to the ranch. "I haven't seen the festival site."

"Neither have I."

"I'm surprised," she said. "Didn't you go check on the damage after the tornado hit?"

"No."

"Would you like to come along?"

She was surprised when he didn't answer right away. He'd always been restless and up for anything.

"I guess I'd better take advantage of my freedom for as long as I can."

Asher wasn't feeling particularly chatty during the three-hour car ride to Mustang Point, an elite waterside community with a large marina in Trinity Bay. Because Appaloosa Island was only accessible by helicopter and boat—a ferry crossed to the island daily—the Edmond family kept several boats for their own use.

The investigators had returned his car and Asher

had insisted he drive. The luxury sedan was far more comfortable for a road trip than Lani's utilitarian SUV. Plus, with him behind the wheel, she could spend the trip working on her laptop. If she noticed his reserve, she gave no sign. Which, of course, only fueled his frustration.

Being investigated by his ex-lover was bad enough. That his father had been the one to hire her cut deep. And how could he talk to her about how betrayed he felt without plunging deep into the complex emotional crap that defined his relationship with Rusty?

Maybe he should just go ahead and tell her what was really going on. Why he'd quit polo and gone to work for The Edmond Organization. More than any time before, he wanted her to know the man he truly was. For her to choose to have faith in him. To recognize that not only was he innocent of stealing the festival funds, but that he would never in a million years stoop to something so low.

And what if he told her everything and it didn't change her perception? He sensed that it was habit for her to regard him with a jaundiced eye. As with his adoptive father, she found it easier to write him off. To her, he would remain "frat boy" and his pride rejected having to prove that he was no longer that guy.

They had lunch at the marina restaurant before heading to the dock. The forty-foot boat that Asher had been staying on when he first met Lani had been replaced by a sixty-foot model that handled like a dream. He keyed in the code to unlock the double-glass doors and swept his arm in a grand gesture for her to precede him inside. Far from looking pleased by his gallantry, she shot him a repressive frown before entering the comfortable cabin with panoramic views from the wraparound windows.

The sleek open space held a lounge area with a comfortable sectional couch and a large well-appointed kitchen with tons of countertop space for food prep and an eat-in banquette.

"Are you thirsty?" he asked, determined to play the part of a good host. "The boat is fully stocked with everything you could ever want."

Her eyebrow arched at that. "I'll take a sparkling water if you have it."

"I know we do." Practically everything Gina drank had to have bubbles. "We also have that jalapeño vodka you like so well. I make sure the boat is stocked with it. You know, just in case…"

Her lips parted as if she wanted to ask, *In case of what?* But she settled for shaking her head in disapproval before continuing to survey the elegant surroundings.

"This looks new," she murmured as he pulled out glasses, filling them with ice and a slice of lime.

Still annoyed that she'd had dinner with his father the night before and refused to tell him why or what they'd discussed, he shot back, "Is that your way of asking me if I used the festival funds to buy a new boat?"

"You need to take this more seriously." She regarded him steadily as he poured sparkling water over the ice. "You're in big trouble and flippant remarks like that are not making my job any easier."

He coped with stress by making light of things. *Never let them see you sweat.* No one knew the amount of anger, insecurity or frustration he'd bottled up over the years. But he'd learned that if you play the part of someone unbothered by problems, then those difficulties have less of a chance of wearing you down.

"I didn't steal the funds and the boat doesn't belong to me." Summoning a weary half smile, Asher held the glass out to her. "But you already know that." For several seconds the only sound in the space was the happy explosions of a hundred tiny bubbles. "I'm not the villain here."

He could probably say it a million times and she'd never believe him until the truth came out, proving his innocence. What he wouldn't give for someone, anyone—but *especially* her—to believe he wasn't a thieving asshole.

His patience was rewarded when she stepped forward to accept it and their fingers grazed, sending an electric current of longing through him. Lust flared, compelling and dangerous. If he took her in his arms and kissed her the way he wanted to, they would be naked and on the floor in minutes.

But passion was easy. It was the moments in between that made a relationship grow and flourish. Or fail miserably. Whatever came, he wanted a shot with Lani.

Reacting to his volatile mood, she sipped her water in silence.

"I mean," he continued mercilessly, "if I were to steal millions of dollars, I wouldn't spend it on a boat or a house in the Maldives. I'd choose someplace more interesting than some remote island to buy real estate."

Lani studied him. "I don't get you."

"I assure you, I am quite simple to understand."

"Maybe once." She spun away from him, gliding toward the open glass doors that led to the semi-circular couch off the back of the boat. "I'm not sure I believe that anymore."

Asher trailed after her. "What's changing your mind? Am I wearing you down with my incessant claims of innocence?"

Suddenly he saw the clever trap he'd made for himself. Although it was in his best interest to convince her that he hadn't stolen the money, as soon as he stopped being a suspect, she'd be off chasing new leads. And he wasn't ready to let her walk out of his life just yet.

"Never mind." She rubbed her temple. "I must be tired. I don't know what I'm saying anymore." Still, she gave him a long searching look before speaking again. "Should we be going?"

"Don't you want a tour of the yacht first?"

"It's a boat. I'm sure I can find my way around if I need to."

"There's two state rooms," he narrated as if she hadn't already shut him down. "You can have your pick, although I have to say the views from the one in the stern are much better."

She looked surprised, and then worried. "This is a day trip. Out and back. We're not staying here overnight."

"I thought it'd be fun." His smile was all innocence. "For old times' sake."

Bright color burned in her cheeks at his words even as outrage made her eyes snap in irritation. Her spine stiffened as she seemed to gather breath to deliver whatever scathing rebuttal she hoped would shut him down.

His remark hadn't been the least bit suggestive, but she certainly took it that way. *Interesting.* Obviously she was remembering how things had been between them all those years before.

"Is there a problem?" He continued before she could argue. "I mean we're living in close quarters at the ranch. It's not different if you're alone with me here, is it?"

"Of course not," she shot back. "I just thought we'd head to the festival site and then go back to Royal. I wasn't planning on making a night of it."

"It was a long drive. Let's just spend the night and head back tomorrow."

"I didn't pack for an overnight stay," she reminded him.

"Not to worry, Gina always keeps an assortment of clothes on board. I'm sure she wouldn't mind if you borrowed something."

"I guess we can spend the night." She gave in with a grimace, looking less sure of herself by the minute.

"Great." Asher didn't put too much energy into his voice, not wanting her to realize how delighted he was to have won this standoff. "I'll start the engine and then cast off the lines."

"I've got it."

Five years earlier they'd spent a lot of time together on the previous yacht and she was familiar with the routine. Still, Asher was surprised when she headed for the mooring lines and began removing each one from the cleats. He'd been out on a variety of boats with a lot of women, but none of them lifted a finger to help. They believed their contribution was to parade around in bikinis, providing eye candy. While he wasn't opposed to beautiful, scantily clad women, he'd always appreciated Lani's helpfulness. Just another way she stood out in his mind.

To his surprise, she came up to the bridge as he reversed the yacht out of the slip. One level above the lounge, the fly bridge came equipped with top-of-the-line electronics and offered impressive views. Asher registered disappointment as Lani settled into the spacious seating area to his left. Seriously, what had he expected? She wasn't about to come snuggle beside him the way she used to back in the day. Forcibly tamping down his emotions, he navigated out of the marina and pointed the sixty-foot yacht into the bay.

The distance from the marina to the festival site on Appaloosa Island was a quick fifteen-minute trip. They'd chosen to locate the event on the undeveloped side of the island, far from the resort where Asher and Lani had met for the first time and away from the expensive homes that lined the waterfront.

Despite his initial excitement over the festival, after the preliminary idea generation and brainstorming sessions, he'd left the organizing to others and focused on the vendors. He'd been involved in several charity events during his years of playing polo and endorsements were a big part of that. Plus, his family had rejected many of the suggestions he'd made about the location and vision for the festival, leaving him feeling less and less connected to the nuts-and-bolts aspect of organizing the event. When he'd stopped attending board meetings, no doubt his family had chalked it up to yet another time that Asher failed to follow through on something. But he had a hard time sticking with anything when his heart wasn't in it.

As the boat neared the festival grounds, his gaze swept over the ruin of what had been the hopes and dreams of so many. His stomach gave a sickening wrench. No wonder everyone hated him.

Five

As the boat idled past the festival site's devastation, Lani kept her attention fixed on Asher's face. Convinced she'd glimpse something that would establish he'd been guilty all along, her righteous triumph faded as his shock and horror never wavered. The torment in his eyes as he gazed over buildings wrecked by the tornado made her throat tighten.

The dock had been spared, but Asher made no attempt to head that way. Instead he moved parallel to shore and pushed a button on the control panel. A muffled thunk reached her ears and then the floor beneath her feet began to vibrate as the anchor chain emptied from the hold.

"What are you doing?" she asked, shivering at the grim set of his expression.

"Anchoring," came his clipped answer.

When they'd first met, she'd viewed Asher as a charming libertine, engaged in an unending pursuit of entertainment. And watching him now as he skillfully maneuvered the giant yacht, she was reminded of how in the early days of getting to know him, his easy confidence with everything he did had won her over. She was a woman whose self-reliance had been encouraged by her parents. And was used to doing things for herself. So, sitting back and relying on someone else for a change had been a unique and thrilling experience and one she still struggled with.

"There's no way we can tie up to that dock." His attention appeared fixed on the process of making sure the anchor latched onto the floor of the bay, but a frown appeared as he shot glances toward the island. "Even if I trusted that the storm hadn't damaged the dock, it wasn't built for boats this size. What happened to the one that could accommodate twenty or more yachts?"

The answer was so obvious that Lani just stared at Asher in bemusement. She couldn't process how genuinely baffled he looked. Her instincts told her he was utterly mystified, but how was that possible? He would've been involved with the festival organization from the start. Didn't he know what had been going on here?

"Or did they manage to build it and it was destroyed by the tornado?" He continued to voice his troubled thoughts out loud.

At moments like these, moments like when he lavished his attention on his string of polo horses, dedicating himself to their health and welfare, she questioned if he was as irresponsible as he seemed.

"As far as I know, this was the only dock that was

ever built," Lani said, her voice gentler than she'd meant it to be.

Once he seemed satisfied that the anchor was secure, he shut off the motor and remained where he was, staring at the shore. "So many people were counting on the festival," he murmured. "We'd promised to fund Valencia Donovan's horse rescue charity with a portion of the proceeds from the festival ticket sales. She was going to expand her property and start an equine therapy program. And I know Rafe Cortez-Williams took out a second mortgage on his restaurant to invest in the festival." He screwed his eyes shut and rubbed his face. "With all the losses they're facing, it's selfish of me to think only about my problems. But someone set me up. Someone close to me. I feel so betrayed." The anguish in his voice tore at her.

"I'm sorry this is happening to you," she said, the words coming before she'd considered them.

Asher's dismay was getting to her. And that couldn't be allowed to happen. Feeling sorry for him was the wrong way to go. This was his fault, after all. *He* caused this problem when he stole the money. Which meant he didn't deserve her sympathy or support. He'd done a terrible thing and ruined countless lives.

Yet if this were true, why did she keep falling for his denials? If she was so convinced of his guilt, shouldn't she be able to see right through his excuses? Granted, it had been ages since she'd last seen him, but why would he have done something so obvious? He had to know he was going to get caught. Asher might be reckless, but he wasn't an idiot. What was his endgame? She recalled his reaction when she told him about the house in the Maldives. He'd genuinely looked clueless as to where that was.

"Come on."

"How are we going to get over there?" She looked at the thirty or so feet of open water between the boat and the dock.

"We could swim."

"I don't have a suit."

"I'm sure one of Gina's bikinis would fit you."

His gaze drifted down her body, a slow, lazy leer that made her skin pebble at the thought of his hands trailing over her flesh. Despite the afternoon's humidity, she shivered. It wasn't fair that the man could turn her on with a mere look. But the heat moving into her cheeks wasn't fired by irritation. It kindled as she recalled other afternoons when they'd swum together off these waters while golden sunlight sparkled on the blue surface. And she'd never forget that one night when they'd gone skinny-dipping, clad in nothing but moonlight. Asher had licked the cool salty water droplets off her naked breasts as he'd dipped his fingers into the slippery heat between her legs. The memory of that encounter hit her like a freight train and Lani's hands began to shake.

Coming here had been a bad idea. She'd brought him to the island to face reality. To show him the damage he'd caused. Instead, he'd reacted in a way that made him seem more victim than villain. She'd lost control of the situation and the only person learning a lesson here was her.

He was dangerous. To the people around him who he'd stolen from, and to her own peace of mind. She'd spent years telling herself that she'd been a fool to be taken in by Asher Edmond. Time and distance had allowed her to believe that she'd never be misled by him again. Yet here she was lost in the past, remembering only the good times and doubting what she knew to be true. That Asher had a knack for telling people what they wanted to hear and making them believe he was a better man than he actually was. Or was that just her wounded heart talking?

"Isn't there some sort of a dinghy we can take over to the island? I don't feel like swimming."

Asher regarded her silently for a moment. The lush sweep of his lashes shadowed his brown eyes, making his expression hard to read. Lani tried not to think about how much she loved that soft fringe tickling her skin or how the raspy glide of his stubble over the sensitive area where her shoulder and neck connected had driven her mad with desire. She'd been so weak back then, so susceptible to every sensation Asher visited upon her inexperienced body. Was it any wonder she'd fallen head over heels for him when he given her such pleasure? When every grace of his fingertips or the heat of his gaze could set off a maelstrom of unquenchable yearning.

"The dinghy it is," he said, his matter-of-fact tone at odds with the questing weight of his gaze.

When he turned away toward the ladder that descended from the fly deck to the main level, Lani sagged. Only as he disappeared below did she realize she'd been using all her strength to withstand the pull of longing he evoked.

Asher used a crane mounted on the bow to lower the dinghy into the water. As he worked, the wind caught the edges of his unbuttoned shirt and spread it wide. Lani ogled his lean, muscular torso, all too aware that the familiar surroundings were triggering long-buried emotions. Fighting to quell her rioting hormones, she joined Asher at the back of the boat where a swim platform extended off the stern. He'd maneuvered the small inflatable there and tied it to the structure.

"Give me your hand," he said. "The dinghy is a little unsteady."

She waved him off. "I've got this."

"You know," he began, his tone tight and impatient, "you could let me take care of you."

To her dismay, Lani's skin flushed. The first time they'd made love Asher had calmed her nerves by whispering, *Let me care of you.* And then he proceeded to do just that. She'd had a half-dozen orgasms that night, mind-blowing explosions of pleasure that he'd given her. Afterward, she'd been grateful to have been initiated into the physical act of love with that level of expertise. Unfortunately starting off with such an outstanding lover had its downside. Since then, numerous disappointing sexual experiences had followed with men who were not Asher.

Lani stiffened her spine, refusing to let him get to her again. How could she claim to be a professional if spending two days with her ex-lover turned her into a pile of needy mush?

Determined to avoid touching him again and risk revisiting the longing for still more physical contact, Lani ignored Asher's hand, choosing to board the dinghy unassisted. What began as an inelegant clamber onto the inflatable's unstable surface ended in a scene out of a rom-com when the wobbly craft shifted as she stood with one foot in it and one on the swim platform. The next thing Lani knew, she was off balance and pitching sideways. Her shoulder hit the edge of the structure. Pain shot through her as cold water closed over her head. Shock held her in its grasp for several immobilizing seconds before the need for air awakened in her lungs. Lani swept her arms out and down, wincing as the movement sent a sharp twinge through her bruised shoulder.

She surfaced, gasping and splashing, only to be hauled unceremoniously out of the water by big strong hands. Her butt settled onto the swim platform with a thump. She blinked water from her eyes and became aware that Asher cupped her head with one hand while the fingers of his other whisked drops from her cheeks.

"Are you okay?" His deep voice held an unexpected hint of panic that warmed her faster than the hot August sun.

The urge to cry rose up in her so fast that she gasped in dismay. She hated that Asher's concern for her made her feel weak and fragile. She was a street-smart private investigator, prepared for any and all emergencies. Not some silly female who needed a man to take care of her. Yet damned if she didn't appreciate being rescued by Asher. Even if it was his fault in the first place that she'd fallen in.

Scowling, she pushed Asher's hands away. "Leave me alone. I'm fine."

He opened his mouth as if to argue, but then the corners of his eyes crinkled as mirth replaced worry. He pressed his lips together as his shoulders began to shake with suppressed laughter. Lani glared at him in rapidly escalating indignation as she sat in her sopping wet clothes, overcome by embarrassment.

"It isn't funny," she snapped, shoving her palm into his shoulder, taking her discomfort out on him. "And it was all your fault that I fell in."

"Not true. If you'd let me help you into the boat, none of this would've happened." His amusement dimmed. Beneath bold dark eyebrows, his gaze became somber and intense. "Too bad you're always so determined to reject assistance."

"You say that like it's a bad thing that I rely on myself."

"It's not a bad thing to rely on yourself, but when you can't let yourself count on anyone else, then it stops being something positive."

Stung, she jumped on offense. "I don't think you're the best person to give advice on how I should act."

His face wore a mask of bland indifference. "You're probably right." He held out his hand. "Want to try again?"

"You go. I'm going to dry off."

With a brief shrug, he nimbly stepped into the dinghy and untied it. Lani huddled in her wet clothes and shivered, watching as Asher started the outboard and steered the inflatable toward the island.

Asher roamed the festival site for an hour, barely able to process how the whole damned thing had gone so wrong. Even without the tornado damage, the missing funds meant a lot of people had been ruined. If not for the storm, it wouldn't have come out that no payment had been made to the insurance company that was supposed to protect them against such a tragedy. Yet even before the winds had ripped apart buildings and uprooted trees, the festival had been sabotaged. How could things have gotten so bad?

And who in the hell had set him up for stealing the money?

It had to be someone close to him, or someone actively involved in the festival organization. He just couldn't imagine anyone he knew doing something so nefarious. Or who might have been opportunistic enough to embezzle. Obviously Lani was an expert at these sorts of investigations, but with her gaze focused directly on him, how hard would she look at anyone else?

In a grim mood, Asher returned to the boat. Lani was nowhere to be found so he headed into the lounge, poured himself two fingers of whiskey and shot back the alcohol. As the spirits seared his chest, warming his whole body, he closed his eyes and reviewed the day's events.

Lani so clearly believed he was the villain. And frankly, after looking at everything that had been done and scrutinizing the financials, he was starting to see why everyone thought he'd stolen the money. Nor did his current situation inspire anyone to give him the benefit of the doubt. He was living at his father's estate, working in a job that had been handed to him because of his connection to Rusty. He had little that he hadn't been given. It didn't cast him in the most flattering light. One thing was for sure, his current predicament was a major wake-up call. He'd given Rusty two years at The

Edmond Organization. Time to make a new plan and dive into his future.

That is, if he *had* a future. The way things were going, it was looking pretty likely that he'd have many years behind bars to ponder the errors of his ways and figure out a better way to go forward.

He didn't realize his eyes remained closed until he felt a stirring in the air and realized he was no longer alone in the lounge. Pushing out a steadying breath, he got his expression back under control and opened his eyes.

Lani stepped into the kitchen and leaned against the cabinet near the sink with her arms crossed. She wore a pair of tropical-print wide-leg pants with a shoulder-baring crop top in royal blue. Her bare toenails peeked from beneath the flowing hem. Although the resort wear suited Lani, it also stripped away the professional veneer that made her so attractive to him.

She was a woman of substance, someone he valued for her authenticity, her intelligence and her drive. In so many ways they were complete opposites. She was focused and organized. While he tended to careen through life, moving from one experience to another.

"Are you planning on getting drunk?" she asked, glancing pointedly at the tumbler in his hand.

"Don't you think I deserve to?" Since he was still standing by the bar, he poured himself another shot of whiskey and then began to accumulate the ingredients for Lani's spicy margarita. "Feel like joining me? There's an icemaker there." He indicated the stainless-steel door beside the beverage cooler. "And you'll find limes and fresh jalapeños in the fridge beside it. I'm afraid you'll have to do with off-the-shelf sweet-and-sour mix, but in that cabinet you'll find chili salt."

"This isn't a party," Lani said, crossing her arms over her chest and refusing to move. "We're here on business."

"And you've never met a client over drinks?" Like the night before when she'd dined with his father at the Texas Cattleman's Club.

"You're not a client. And I don't think you should be drinking."

"Too late." He toasted her with his glass, downed the whiskey and lifted the bottle once more.

She was right to say he shouldn't be drinking. The alcohol wouldn't help defuse the tension in his gut put there by what he'd seen on the island. Nor could it dim his urgent pleasure at having her back in his life even under these terrible circumstances. As for diminishing the temptation to cross the room, wrap his arms around her and slide his lips onto the strong pulse in her throat...

"Lani." He lowered his chin and blinked slowly as warmth raced through his veins. She was so beautiful. He'd missed the way she crossed her arms and glared at him. Or how she looked so sleepy and sweet in the mornings. The corners of his mouth curled up in a slow grin. "Do you remember how we loved to picnic on the boat, make love all night and then have breakfast in bed the next morning?"

"Stop it right now." She leveled her finger at him. "I'm not doing this with you. We are not going to sleep together."

Her lips said no, but her eyes weren't quite as convincing.

"Because you don't want to?" he taunted. "Or because it would be unprofessional?"

"Both."

"I don't believe you." He spoke each syllable with deliberate care so she wouldn't miss his point.

"I don't care what you believe." She glowered at him a little too aggressively. "It's the truth."

Wondering what it would take to get her back on his side, Asher raked his hand through his hair. Once upon a time he'd been able to convince her to take a chance on him by capitalizing on the sizzling sexual energy that exploded between them whenever they touched. Yet while hormones had raged during those sultry summer months they spent together, he'd gotten the impression that he was some sort of curiosity to her. The good girl wanted to walk on the wild side just once before settling down to a career steeped in rules and regulations.

"Is it the truth?" he demanded, tired of her denials. "Or is that what you tell yourself at night when sleeping all alone in your bed?"

These words were not at all what he wanted to say to her, but with frustration and longing a tangled knot inside his gut, hollow charm lost out to desperate honesty.

"You're so sure I'm sleeping alone?" She was so obviously bluffing that he almost smiled.

"Yes," he said, chest tightening as she scowled at him. "Am I wrong? Have you found somebody that gets you?" Because he hoped she wouldn't settle for anything less.

Needing something to do, Asher moved into the

kitchen. He ignored her obvious show of maintaining a safe distance from him as he opened the refrigerator and pulled out the produce he'd mentioned earlier. Finding a cutting board and a sharp knife, he gestured for her to join him. Then he began fixing a spicy margarita just the way she liked it.

"Someone who gets me." She gave a rough laugh as she rinsed the jalapeño, before picking up the knife. "Don't act as if you give a damn about my love life."

Asher's mouth went dry. He took a step in her direction and lowered his voice. "Of course I give a damn. I want you to be happy—"

"Don't." She whirled on him with a twelve-inch blade extended in his direction. He gulped. The stainless steel glinted wickedly in her hand. Her stormy eyes practically begged him to say more. "Don't pretend that you care. I'm not going to fall for you ever again."

Fall for you.

Five years earlier he hadn't understood what he was doing when he'd relentlessly pursued her. At first she'd been a challenge. Resisting him at every turn. Refusing to give him a chance. Reluctant to let him in. And even when he'd broken through her well-fortified defenses, she'd kept the key to her heart well hidden.

Until the lazy summer days began to grow short and he realized he didn't want to lose her. He'd invited her to come to Argentina for the polo season and she'd told him that she loved him, but that she couldn't give up on grad school. He'd been terrified by the gift she'd offered him and clueless how to keep their good thing going now that the summer fling had turned into a serious romance.

"I did care about you," he countered, shaken by the mistake he'd made all those years ago when he'd chosen his freedom over her love.

"Oh, please. I watched you hit on women for a week before you even noticed me."

She looked plenty put out that she hadn't been his first choice. Except that wasn't the case at all. From the moment he had spotted her waiting on adjacent tables, he'd been mesmerized. He just hadn't been ready for the emotions that had slammed into him. Lust he could handle. Longing had caught him by surprise.

"What do you want to hear? That you were unlike any other woman I'd ever met and I didn't know how to handle that?"

"I'm only interested in what's real," she declared, slicing the lime with malevolent force.

"That is the truth." But he could see from her ramrod-straight spine that nothing he could say would convince her.

"Just be straight with me." She set the knife down and shot him a hard look. "Tell me where you put the money. That's the only truth I'm interested in hearing."

Six

"Where are we off to today?" Asher asked the morning day after their impromptu visit to Appaloosa Island. If she'd hoped that compelling him to confront the damage to the island would provoke his confession about the missing funds, she'd been completely wrong. While he'd seemed disturbed by all he'd seen, he hadn't confessed or behaved in a way that confirmed his guilt.

Lani scanned his handsome face, fighting the sheer enjoyment of his gorgeous smile and ready energy. Yet even as she fell into the trap of wanting to do whatever made him happy, she recognized that he could be putting on an act.

She searched for evasion in his lively brown eyes, but saw only genuine curiosity and good-natured enthusiasm. It sucked that she no longer trusted her own judgment. Five years ago, his ability to twist her emo-

tions and make her lose control of her sensibilities had
almost been her ruin. Fortunately, she'd woken up just
in time. While turning down his invitation to go with
him to Argentina had been the hardest decision she'd
ever made, no good would've come from giving up her
carefully crafted plans. And Lani was convinced that
even if she'd followed Asher Edmond into an uncertain
future, they never would've lasted. So what if her days
weren't as bright and shining without him in it. Look
at how he'd ended up. Eventually he would've dragged
her down with him.

"*I'm* going to visit Abby Carmichael," she said, em-
phasizing the first-person singular pronoun. Letting
him help with this investigation was a really bad idea.

"Abby… Carmichael. The name is familiar."

"She was filming a documentary on the festival."

"Oh, sure, she interviewed all of us." Asher arched
his eyebrows. "What's your interest in her?"

"She has footage of what was going on with the festival."

"What do you think you'll find on it?" His lips
twisted into a sardonic quirk. "Video of me sneaking
off with bags of money and burying them in the sand
somewhere?"

Although he spoke in a light, mocking tone, Lani
recognized his dark humor masked concern. Her time
training to be an FBI agent hadn't been a waste. In those
moments when she could put her emotional response to
him aside, she saw his anxiety clearly.

"That would be really helpful," she responded, arching her eyebrows at him. "Especially if they are marked

with big dollar signs, indicating that the bags are full of cash."

As her not-so-witty repartee made him relax, Lani sighed in weary frustration with herself. She came out of her thoughts and caught Asher regarding her intently. It was in moments like these when she glimpsed his somber watchfulness that she knew there was more to this man than he let people see.

"Can I come along?" he asked. "Maybe a third set of eyes could be helpful."

Against her better judgment, Lani found herself nodding. "Sure, why not."

Why did she keep pandering to his needs? What was she *thinking*? That if they could work the investigation together, then maybe they'd have some sort of shot in the future?

He wasn't good for her. Once she got him out of this situation, she'd probably never hear from him again. The thought made her heart clench. Five years ago she'd foolishly believed if she told him that school was important to her, then he would agree to try the long-distance thing. She'd hoped that maybe by the time she graduated, he would've settled down and their differences would've stopped being an issue.

But clearly fate had other things in store for them both.

"Thanks." He looked as if he wanted to say more, but then just gave her a smile that didn't quite reach his eyes.

Before she acted on her need to reassure him, Lani grabbed her jacket and headed for the apartment door. Before she could reach it, Asher was there, gazing down at her with his most-earnest expression. The heady scent of his cologne encircled her, causing an uptick in her pulse.

"I really mean it," he said, fingertips skimming her arm. The light contact aroused a flood of longing, but if it showed on her face, he didn't appear to notice. "It means the world to me that you are giving me the benefit of the doubt."

I'm not...

She might've been able to resist if he'd swept her into a passionate embrace and kissed her with wild abandon. Bracing against his onslaught of sensual persuasion was her first instinct. Instead, her steely resolve was being chipped away by his fleeting touches, the unexpected flashes of sincerity, his apparent gratitude that she was going to bat for him because she believed in his innocence. Guilt swept through her. Did he recognize how little she trusted him? Or did he think his tactics were working?

"Asher..."

Before she could figure out what she planned on telling him, he dropped the sweetest, lightest, most-affectionate kiss on her lips. The gentle pressure came and went so fast it was like being kissed by a butterfly, but she doubted her whole body would've lit up from a glancing brush of gossamer wings.

"It's enough that you're letting me come along." He swallowed her fingers in his warm, strong hand and drew her out the door. "You don't need to warn me that I'm still suspect number one. It's just nice to have some control over my fate."

A warning trembled on her lips. He had no control

whatsoever. But his optimistic expression overwhelmed her caution. Why crush his hopes when there was nothing concrete to do the stomping?

Instead she gave his fingers a quick squeeze and said, "Let's go."

The day before she'd made this appointment to meet with Abby Carmichael at Carter Crane's ranch. Two months earlier the filmmaker had arrived to capture background on the town, the Edmond family and many of those participating in the Soiree on the Bay festival.

Lani had heard that the couple was an opposites-attract pair who'd met and fallen in love in the midst of the festival development. Abby was a city girl. Carter a rancher. Lani couldn't help but compare the couple's romantic destiny to what had happened between her and Asher. While Abby had moved to Royal, letting romance upended her world, Lani had sacrificed her personal life in favor of her career. She was eager to see how Abby was faring in the aftermath of her decision.

The woman who answered the door had long straight dark hair, inquisitive brown eyes, and a beautiful light brown complexion. A cropped white T-shirt and skinny jeans showed off her lean body and her smile was positively gleeful as her gaze landed on Asher.

"I don't suppose I could get you to sit for another interview."

Lani stiffened protectively. She'd forgotten that word around town was that Abby intended to change the focus of her documentary to an exposé on the failed festival and the scandalous missing funds.

"Maybe after I'm exonerated," Asher replied with a

suave grin that made Lani's toes curl even though she wasn't on the receiving end of his attention.

"You don't think he's guilty?" Abby's eyes went wide as her gaze bounced between Asher and Lani.

"I'm investigating the missing festival funds," she said, irritation firing as she reminded the filmmaker of the reason they were here.

She knew better than to let her personal feelings for Asher get in the way of doing her job. No matter how bad the case looked against him, she had blurred the lines between doing the job Kingston Blue had hired her for and saving her former lover from jail. That the two missions might be on a parallel course would only work for her as long as Asher was innocent.

"May we see the footage?" Lani prompted.

"Of course," Abby demurred, leading them toward a large workstation with several monitors, keyboards and other computer equipment. "I pulled footage from the various visits to the island with the organizers of the event. I also have interviews with everyone involved." Her gaze flicked to Asher. "Any idea what you're looking for?"

The massive volume of video the documentarian had recorded was overwhelming. But helpful.

"Let's start with the footage from the visits to the island."

Abby began scrolling through various files, clicking on several in search of what she was looking for. "There are a lot of people involved. Between the Edmond family, the construction crew, marketers, food vendors. The list goes on and on…"

With the embezzlement evidence pointing directly at

Asher, the investigators had stopped searching for other suspects and begun building a case against him. No one else would be looking at what Abby had recorded.

To Lani's mind, the people who were closest to the Edmond family were at the top of her list of suspects. Specifically Ross Edmond. Despite Asher's assurance that his brother couldn't have stolen the money, and then taken the extra step of framing Asher, Lani intended on taking a good look at him.

"That's odd," Asher murmured.

Lani braced herself for whatever had caught his eye. She'd worried that even if there was nothing of interest in what Abby had filmed, Asher would create some sort of distraction that would lead her down a divergent tunnel. His specialty was deflection and the man had a knack for getting inside her head. Who knew what crazy theory she would be chasing next if he got his way.

But it was Abby, and not Lani, that took the bait. "What's odd?"

"I wasn't along on this particular visit to the festival site." He turned to Abby. "Can you run this back about ten minutes?"

"Sure."

"Look." The footage that had caught Asher's attention was a shot of Rusty and Ross walking the grounds, looking relaxed in each other's company. From the state of the building going on and the lack of a rift between the father and son, the footage must've been shot several months earlier.

"What are we looking for?" Abby asked eagerly and Lani was happy to let her lead.

Asher hesitated before answering, his focus locked on the monitor. "That." He pointed to a corner of the screen where Billy Holmes appeared. Although at first his expression appeared innocuous, on closer viewing, his charming veneer had slipped, replaced by a cold glare.

"He's staring at Ross and Rusty like they've done something to annoy him," Asher said, sounding triumphant. "Which is strange because I've never ever seen him looking anything but absolutely pleased with himself."

Wow. Interesting indeed.

"Well, he certainly isn't looking so happy there." Asher sounded intrigued. "How much more footage is there of this day?"

While Abby and Asher leaned forward, scanning the images on the monitor, Lani pondered this new development. Was this a significant lead or just a red herring?

"You know, when I interviewed Billy around the time that this was shot, he let it slip that some money was unaccounted for from the accounts." Abby turned in her chair and faced Asher. "He said the oddest thing. He called it a family matter and then said that *we're* handling it." She emphasized the inclusive pronoun. "He acted very protective of Ross. At the time I just thought it was because they were such good friends." Abby's gaze strayed back to the monitor and a dent appeared between her eyebrows.

Lani had never considered Billy as a suspect because he hadn't had access to the festival accounts. But she remembered Kingston Blue's theory that Ross was involved. Could they be in on it together?

If so, why did it upset Billy that Ross and Rusty seemed to be getting along?

They spent another hour reviewing footage, but nothing else jumped out. Nevertheless Lani asked Abby for copies of whatever she had featuring the Edmond family and Billy, including the individual interviews with the Edmonds.

Following the meeting with Abby Carmichael, Lani was in a thoughtful mood as they headed back to Elegance Ranch. Asher was wondering if he was being too optimistic to think that he was starting to see cracks forming in the thick wall of doubt Lani had constructed to keep him at bay.

"Weird about the way Billy was glaring at Ross and Rusty," he muttered as his curiosity grew too overwhelming to bear in silence. "What do you suppose that means?"

She took one hand off the steering wheel and rubbed her temple as if trying to alleviate pain. "I don't know."

But by watching her, seeing the telltale tightening of her lips and a slight indent between her brows, she obviously *did* know, and whatever was bothering her had caused some sort of shift in perception. Hope blared in him like a car alarm. Could she be coming around to believing that he hadn't stolen the money?

"I had no idea Billy was the one spreading word of missing funds," Asher said, continuing to chew on one of the many disturbing things he'd discovered today. "I mean, what did he think he was doing? He had to know the news would hurt our family."

"Explain to me again about Billy's relationship with

Ross and how he came to be living in one of the guest-houses on the estate."

"He and Ross were good buds in college," Asher told her. "He showed up in Royal a couple years ago. As to why he's living in the guesthouse…" He thought back. "Rusty took to him right away." He made no effort to hide the bitterness in his voice. "I guess all it takes to get on Rusty's good side is to kiss his ass twenty-four/seven. Billy's an expert at that."

"You don't like him."

Asher had a ready answer. "Do I sound like a jerk if I admit that it bugs me that this guy comes out of no-where and gets my dad to like him when I've spent my whole life waiting for Rusty to acknowledge me for doing a good job at anything?"

"I think you are justified to want Rusty's attention. He's the only father you've ever known. It makes sense that you want him to be proud of you."

Venting about being slighted by his father left Asher feel like he'd been kicked in the gut. Sharing that hadn't been easy and he appreciated Lani's empathic response. They didn't talk until she stopped the SUV behind the barn.

Asher turned to her as something electric and pow-erful sizzled in the air between them. "Are you heading back to Dallas right away or can you stay for dinner?"

The festival case wasn't the only one she was work-ing. Lani was helping several clients.

"I have time for dinner."

Five words that flooded him with excitement. "Great."

She preceded him up the stairs to his apartment and

keyed in the code. At her urging, he'd started locking his door. Until she came along, he hadn't considered that his stuff or his person could be in danger and her insistence on security was adorable. He didn't want her to think he wasn't taking her seriously, but the truth was, the only thing of value worth locking up was his heart and the more time he spent with her, the less confident he was at being able to keep it safe.

"Pour me a shot of whiskey," she said, setting down her laptop and slipping her blazer off her shoulders. "I'll be right back."

Asher did as she asked and then began hunting in his refrigerator for what he could use to put together a meal. He had steak and pasta. She liked Gorgonzola cheese. Would she remember the recipe they'd made on the boat that summer?

It wasn't until ten minutes passed that he noticed the water running in the bathroom. She was in the shower, probably thinking through what they'd learned that day. While he waited for her to reemerge, he sipped at his whiskey and stared in the direction of the guesthouse where Billy Holmes stayed.

"Is this mine?"

The sound of her voice broke Asher out of his thoughts. He turned around and the sight of her made the room tilt.

He blinked.

She wore a large blue button-down shirt that had definitely come out of his closet and nothing else. The sight of her pale bare legs and unbound silky black hair made his chest seize. As he stared at her in astonishment, she tipped the crystal tumbler and tossed back the entire contents. He watched her throat as she swallowed the whiskey and savored the widening of her eyes at the impact of the fiery liquid.

Asher wasn't sure if the intensity of his gaze or the liquor put color in her cheeks, but two bright patches appeared over her cheekbones.

"I hope you don't mind but I borrowed one of your shirts," she said. "I jumped into the shower before remembering that I didn't have any clean clothes. I tossed my things in the washer. They'll be clean and dry by the time we're done with dinner."

She was *naked* underneath his shirt? Damn it. Now he was the one with fire raging in his veins.

"I'm afraid I can't have you wearing my clothes," he joked, somehow managing to maintain a humorous demeanor despite the hunger clawing at him. "Take it off."

He definitely succeeded in surprising her because her lips parted in a soft *O*. It took him a second to realize she didn't intend to complain. Instead her eyebrows rose boldly in answer to his challenge.

She set her hands on her hips. "Did you miss the part where I have nothing else to wear?"

"Don't you think it's rude to take things without asking permission?" he countered, advancing in her direction.

A smile played around her lips, sizzling sweet as she methodically backpedaled toward the hall that led to the bedrooms. His gaze followed the trail of her hand as she slipped one button after another free, baring more creamy skin with each step. She was taunting him, daring him to catch her before she reached the guest bedroom. But he could move faster. That is, until his shirt smacked him in the face, blinding him just long enough for her to disappear.

Instinct took over. He tossed the shirt aside and charged after her. Three enormous strides and he closed in on her. Snatching her around the waist, he lifted her off her feet, intending to haul her into his bedroom. He had to find a bed. *Now.* While her passions were all lit up. Before her brain kicked in.

But the instant her naked body careened against his, he found the first solid surface available and set her back against the wall beside the door leading to the master bedroom.

Sliding one hand under her round butt cheek, he sank his fingers into her soft flesh and lifted her. She latched her arms around his shoulders, encircled his waist with her thighs and flicked her tongue into the sensitive skin beneath. His shoulder muscles bunched as a tsunami of arousal pounded through him.

"I need you to take me right here." She purred the demand against his skin, nipping his neck for emphasis, knowing it would drive him crazy. "Right now."

"Hell, yeah."

Her mouth bashed into his, lips parting, tongue searching. He dove straight into the hungry assault, sucking, kissing, erasing their years spent apart. Her skin grew slick as the tempest burned hot between them. He pulled back, determined to shift them to the bed in his room, but her thighs tightened around him.

"Here and now, frat boy," she taunted, rocking her hips and grinding against his arousal, making him moan.

He lost the will to argue with her. If she wanted it

hard and fast up against the wall, he would give it to her. Later he could spend lazy hours chasing her curves with his fingers and lips, but for now he thought he'd die if he couldn't bury himself in her hot tight heat.

Sliding his hand over her rib cage, he cupped her breast, grazing her tight nipple with his thumb. Her breath grew ragged as he leaned forward, kissing her soft skin where shoulder met neck and trailing his tongue into the hollow of her collarbone. She ground against him, her muscles flexing in a familiar rhythm. He longed to be moving with her, *in* her. She was an addiction he'd never recovered from.

He reached down to unfasten the button holding his jeans closed and slid down the zipper. Her fervent arousal called to him as his dick sprang free. She gyrated wildly, bringing her slick heat into contact with his erection. He was an instant away from plunging into her when the need for protection struck him.

What was he doing? He'd dreamed about a moment like this for nearly five years. Why was he rushing? With her thighs clamped around his body, he spun them both and moved toward the bed. Before they went any further, he needed to get as naked as she was and to make sure she was safe.

She seemed to understand what drove him because as soon as her back touched the mattress, she sat up and began to tear at his shirt. While she stripped it off, he strained toward the nightstand drawer. To his relief, his fingers located a condom on the first try. Skimming off his jeans and boxers, he tore open the wrapper and sheathed himself.

Then he was on her, lips seeking hers, legs tangling,

fingers splayed over her lower back to bring their naked skin together. Her lips were designed for his kisses. He'd memorized every curve until all he had to do was close his eyes and let his imagination run riot.

He nuzzled his lips into her neck as she pushed her bare breasts against his chest. A delicate mewling sound came from her throat as he eased his hand over the gorgeous curve of the nearest one and scraped his fingertips over her tight nipple. His mind was already fast-forwarding to how she would writhe as his mouth closed over the sensitive peak, feeling it turn into a hard pebble as he applied suction. With her slender leg trapped between his, she clung to him, purring with delight as he turned his attention to the other breast.

Her hands moved lazily over his shoulders, palms drifted up his neck before she tunneled her fingers into his hair. He trailed his fingers along her abdomen, letting the tips tickle over her belly in a way that made her squirm. Her thighs parted to let him glide along the crease that hid her sex. He dipped into her slippery wetness, lightly stroked her until she cried out, and then withdrew to circle her clit. Her body quaked as he toyed and teased before retreating. Lost in her pleasure, she trembled and bucked her hips, chanting his name. With each second he grew impossibly harder, but refused to stop what he was doing until she came for him.

"That feels *incredible*," she murmured, her chest heaving. "I'm so close…"

As if that triggered her, Lani threw her head back and howled. She climaxed in a rush. Her muscles tensing. Nails biting into his shoulders. He rubbed himself against her hip, caught up in her pleasure. The explo-

sion that ripped through her was almost strong enough
to take him with her.

He wanted to laugh at the sheer perfection of it, of
her, but he needed her to experience even more. He
slid his finger into her and pressed the heel of his palm
against her clit. Legs spread wide, she thrashed her head
from side to side, drove her mound hard against him
and cried out for more.

Oh. Hell. Yes! This is what he'd missed. His senses
magnified each harsh rasp of her ragged breath, the
scent of her musk mingling with the delicious earthi-
ness of her spicy perfume. Asher smiled as their tongues
danced, the taste of whiskey invigorating his nerve endings. And the way her thighs clamped around him as
she strained toward another orgasm, her smoky gaze
locked with his, set him on fire.

Settling between her thighs in the welcoming cra-
dle that had always felt like coming home, he waited
for her to wrap her arms around his neck before pulling his head down to hers. He had to focus hard on not
slamming into her. Despite her obvious burning need
to meet her body with his, he wanted to remind himself
of the texture of her skin, get his mouth on her breasts
and glide his fingers over her tantalizing curves.

"Asher." His name was an urgent plea.

"Easy," he coaxed. "Let me take care of you."

"I love it when you say that," she whispered fiercely.

Her nails scraped down his spine and sank into his
butt muscles. A curse escaped his lips when she barely
paused before reaching between them. She latched her
fingers onto his aching erection and drew him into contact with her hot, wet arousal.

"Now, Asher. I need you *now*."

He needed her, as well. More than needed. He'd craved this for five long years. Having her beneath him on his bed was a dream come true. The moment deserved as much smoldering all-in passion as he could produce. But the heat between them had a mind of its own and all too soon the head of his shaft was pressed against her tight entrance while she panted inarticulate words of encouragement between breaths. Heavenly voices sang in his head as he thrust into her searing heat. He groaned at the firm clasp of her inner muscles around him and lost himself in the homecoming that was Lani Li.

With the magic of the moment consuming his soul, he began to move inside her. Fanning his fingers and gathering her butt in his palm, he began a slow withdrawal, culminating with a teasing hesitation to drive up anticipation. He waited for her to open her eyes and meet his. She always did this. Every time.

When her lashes lifted, baring her mink-brown gaze, her pure, unapologetic joy was the sexiest thing he'd ever seen. He dusted a kiss across her forehead, before he lowered his chin and grazed her lips with his.

"I've missed this," he whispered. "You have no idea how much."

Her tremulous sigh tickled his jaw. "So have I."

What she did to him was unique and one-of-a-kind. He was on fire and she was the gasoline that turned him into a raging inferno. They moaned together as he plunged into her once again, rejoicing as she took all of him. Stroke after stoke, he dove deep, thrusting

Get up to 4
FREE FABULOUS BOOKS
You Love!

To thank you for being a loyal reader we'd like to send you up to 4 FREE BOOKS, absolutely free.

Just write "YES" on the Loyal Reader Voucher and we'll send you up to 4 Free Books and Free Mystery Gifts, altogether worth over $20, as a way of saying thank you for being a loyal reader.

Try **Harlequin® Desire** books featuring the worlds of the American elite with juicy plot twists, delicious sensuality and intriguing scandal.

Try **Harlequin Presents®** Larger-print books featuring the glamourous lives of royals and billionaires in a world of exotic locations, where passion knows no bounds.

Or **TRY BOTH!**

We are so glad you love the books as much as we do and can't wait to send you great new books.

So don't miss out, return your Loyal Reader Voucher Today!

Pam Powers

LOYAL READER
FREE BOOKS VOUCHER

YES! I Love Reading, please send me up to 4 FREE BOOKS and Free Mystery Gifts from the series I select.

Just write in "YES" on the dotted line below then return this card today and we'll send your free books & gifts asap!

➡ ——— YES ——— ⬅

Which do you prefer?

| ☐ **Harlequin Desire®** 225/326 HDL GRGA | ☐ **Harlequin Presents® Larger Print** 176/376 HDL GRGA | ☐ **BOTH** 225/326 & 176/376 HDL GRGM |

FIRST NAME

LAST NAME

ADDRESS

APT.#

CITY

STATE/PROV.

ZIP/POSTAL CODE

EMAIL ☐ Please check this box if you would like to receive newsletters and promotional emails from Harlequin Enterprises ULC and its affiliates. You can unsubscribe anytime.

HD/HP-520-LR21

◇ HARLEQUIN® Reader Service —Here's how it works:

smoothly while hoarse, hungry cries emanated from her throat.

Shudders slammed through him as desire wrestled for control of his muscles. He struggled to stay present and hold off, fighting to withstand the orgasm bent on claiming him. He needed her to come a second time. He moved harder, changed the angle of his deepening thrusts and watched her strain for her release, her rocking hips driving him mad.

She must've known what he wanted for her because she lifted her head and sank her white teeth into his earlobe. The painful nip sent lightning streaking straight to his groin and shattered his willpower.

"More," she commanded, meeting every one of his nearly frantic thrusts with equally reckless abandon.

This wasn't the Lani Li he knew from these last few weeks. This was a return to the wild, wanton woman he'd known that smoking hot, oh-so-memorable summer. Sex with her had ruined him for anyone else. No one matched her curiosity or her focus. She'd investigated his body and discovered all his pleasure spots with the same level of curiosity she'd shown while attacking the embezzlement case.

Pleasure drove him on. The air around them seemed to waver from the heat pouring off their bodies. He struggled for breath that wasn't there. Still, he persisted. The pounding rhythm of her pants pushing him harder. She thrashed her head from side to side, long hair tangling on her sweaty shoulders. Her legs tightened around him, the strength of the vise letting him know she was close.

Her back arched, head rolling back, baring her throat.

"Come with me." The guttural order spilled from her parted lips.

She possessed just enough air to call his name before her muscles went taut, the rhythmic pulse of her release triggering his own. He wanted to hold off, to push her harder, give her more, but her power over him was too potent. There would be plenty of time later to take her past the fiery edge of satisfaction. Right now it was more important for them to be together in this momentous rejoining of body and soul.

He'd love to say he let himself go, but the truth was she grabbed hold of him and yanked him hard into a bone-jarring, roaring avalanche of satisfaction and unending joy. *She* did this to him. She made him crazy and so incredibly happy.

He collapsed into her arms and caught sight of her blissful smile before he entwined their sated bodies. As their skin cooled in the aftermath, Asher stroked back the hair from her face and let his lips drift over her damp shoulder. He hooked the comforter over both of them and grinned as she snuggled her nose into his throat.

When it was just the two of them like this, he could imagine everything would be okay. He'd just stay focused on that for tonight and enjoy that for a little while his life made sense again.

Seven

With her favorite Lowercase album pouring from Asher's Bluetooth speakers, Lani pushed back from her laptop and rubbed her tired, dry eyes. Over the past week, one lead after another had dried up, including any connection between Ross and the missing funds. Faced with a plethora of dead ends, she'd become aware of a growing panic. Was Asher guilty? Lani hoped not. She wouldn't have renewed their physical relationship if she didn't question the validity of the evidence stacked against him. At least she hoped not. She would hate it if she on the verge of making a colossal mistake.

Between long hours at her computer and late nights in bed with Asher, making up for lost time, she'd been lost in a bubble of work and sex. And Lani couldn't remember the last time she'd been this happy.

"Come on," Asher coaxed, his hands sweeping her

long hair away from her neck so he could glide his lips over her skin. "You've done enough work for one day. I think you should take a break."

"What kind of a break did you have in mind?" She glanced up at him, anticipation making her breathless.

"I have twelve polo ponies in training and they need exercise. Wanna help?"

Lani blinked at him, adjusting to this unexpected development. "Help how?"

"How long has it been since you've been on a horse?"

"A while."

When they first met, he'd been intrigued that she'd been a barrel racer when she was young. He'd persuaded her to take him to visit her parents' hobby farm. Introducing him to her horse had gone a lot smoother than meeting her parents. Once they found out he was a professional polo player, they'd definitely not approved and campaigned for her to break things off.

Maybe part of her recognized that she and Asher were too different to work, but she'd waved away their concern, telling her parents that it was just a summer fling and ignoring their exchanged looks that said they believed otherwise.

"What's *a while*?"

Although her folks hadn't sold her horse, she'd been too invested in starting up her investigation firm to take time for recreation. "A year."

"That's too long. Why don't you throw on your boots and I'll saddle Royal Flush for you. She's the best I have and she'll take care of you."

"I guess I could use a break," she said and went to change her footwear.

When she entered the barn, Lani found he had pulled out two horses and was in the process of saddling one of them. She sidled up to the closest one and extended one of the carrots she'd brought as a treat.

"This is Cactus," Asher said, reaching beneath his horse's belly to snag the end of the girth and buckle it into place. "And Royal Flush."

"Hello, beautiful." She scratched the chestnut's shoulder and felt her lean into the caress. Her own horse always seemed to have an itch at this exact same spot. It made her smile.

Asher slid the halter off the bay and plucked the bridle off his shoulder. He threw the reins over the horse's head and poised the bit against the mare's long yellow teeth.

"You're using a gag bit," Lani murmured, recognizing the three-part bit with two joints. "When I raced, I used something similar because Reggie tended not to bend around the barrels and the gag bit really helped with that."

"The gag bit in polo came into popularity in Argentina because the players there were always looking for ways to improve their game. And they found that this style of bit made the horses more linear and less lateral."

"Do you miss it?" Her question caused Asher to still for a moment.

"Do I miss galloping down the field with seven other guys' mallets whizzing past my head as we pursue a little white ball?" His mocking grin flashed, knocking the breath from her body. "Hell ya, I miss it."

"So why aren't you still doing it?"

"Do you think you can manage an English saddle? Or should I put a Western one on Royal Flush?"

The difference between an English and Western saddle was pretty significant. A Western saddle had a deep secure seat with a substantial horn atop a pommel at the front and a high cantle behind. Weighing upward of twenty-five pounds, the design enabled cowboys to stay firmly seated while on bucking broncos and chasing down erratically moving cattle.

English saddles, on the other hand, were flatter and less bulky by comparison and required the rider to work to stay balanced atop their mount. That being said, because of the reduced weight, it was the saddle of choice for jumpers and polo enthusiasts.

Lani could see the dare in Asher's gaze and knew he was trying to divert her attention from the question she'd asked. Still, she gave her options serious consideration. She'd ridden English before, but never while running full tilt across a polo field or while trying to hit a ball with a mallet.

"I think if I plan to stay on, I'd better take the Western saddle."

Ten minutes later they were leading the horses out of the barn and toward a large fenced field. She'd mistaken it for a turnout before this. Instead the groomed grass indicated that this was Asher's training ground. Out of habit she tested the girth before fitting her foot into the stirrup, making sure it remained snug around Royal Flush's belly.

"You don't trust I can saddle a horse?" he teased, swinging up on the bay with no effort whatsoever.

Lani's muscles protested this unaccustomed exercise

and she grunted at the effort it took to swing her leg over the Thoroughbred's back. Seating herself with an ungainly thump, she shot a glance Asher's way, hoping he hadn't seen her struggle. While Royal Flush stood still despite her awkward landing, Asher had his hands full keeping his own mount in place.

"Reggie loved to hold his breath when I saddled him and I always had to double check the girth after I walked him around a bit."

While Royal Flush stood perfectly still, waiting for Lani to cue her, Cactus was full of impatient energy as she sidestepped and backed up.

"She's new," Asher explained, his calm handling of the antsy equine demonstrating a level of patience and skill that was having a dangerous effect on her hormones. He didn't saw on the reins in an effort to control the horse, but sat quietly letting his legs and seat tell the horse what to do. "I adopted her from Donovan Horse Rescue. She's a former racehorse, purchased by an inexperienced rider and badly neglected before Valencia Donovan got her. I guess she was skin and bones. Valencia thinks she might've been abused. But she's fast and loves to run—it's the slowing and turning that we have to work on."

"How come you have so many horses? I thought a string was two or three."

"That's typical for a hobbyist. Three to four is common for a more serious player and if you're professional, a string can be up to ten."

"Are you training these horses because you're considering going back on the professional circuit again?"

"No, these days I play to give these guys experience. It's hobbyist-level action, but I can't give it up entirely. I enjoy the training far too much." He urged his mount forward and used his head to indicate she should come along.

"So once they're trained, then what?"

"I'll sell. I have several people coming to look at horses over the next week or so."

She could hear the ache in his voice. This wasn't something he was doing lightly.

"Why?"

He gave her question a negligent shrug. "Since it doesn't seem as if my family's going to help me and I'm going to be facing some pretty stiff legal bills, I thought I should generate some cash."

They rode in silence for several minutes while Lani processed Asher's pain.

"Are you ready?" he asked, stroking the bay's sweaty neck. The mare had worked herself into a lather before they'd walked to the end and back.

"Ready?" Lani echoed, unsure what he had in mind.

A second later he and Cactus shot away at a gallop. Lani felt Royal Flush gather herself to follow and keyed the mare. As the ground whizzed by, she realized how much she'd missed this. Losing the battle to contain her excitement, a whoop ripped free. All too soon she had to slow the horse as the far fence loomed.

As she drew back on the reins, the chestnut slowed to a smooth canter. Lani's heart was thundering in her ears and she was sure she was grinning like an idiot from the amusement on Asher's face.

"How did that feel?" he asked, sidestepping his

mount over to the fence where a couple of mallets sat propped against the railing.

Lani was breathing hard from the exertion. "She's really fast."

"Argentinian born and bred. They take their polo ponies seriously down there. I bought her as a two-year-old and trained her. She's the best I've ever owned."

And yet he was selling her because his family refused to help him out. Once again Lani had to withstand the urge to comfort him. Still, she hoped the mare went to a good home.

"Let's see how you do with one of these." He handed her a mallet, his wicked grin on full display. "Head weight on that one is six ounces, which is on the lighter end. You should be able to handle it without problems."

As Lani swung the mallet to get the feel of it, she braced herself against the challenge in Asher's expression. Five years earlier, after discovering a mutual love of climbing, white-water rafting and mountain biking, they'd pushed each other to do all sorts of crazy stunts. Afterward, hyped up on adrenaline and endorphins, they'd fallen upon each other in ravenous desire.

Feeling a familiar tingle between her thighs, Lani shifted in the saddle, but this only pressed her sensitive areas against the leather's firm surface, intensifying the ache there. A breeze blew across her hot skin, and she savored the cooling caress. Damn it! The man could get her hot and bothered just by being in the same vicinity.

She was glad when Asher started demonstrating the finer arts of polo. Riding a horse while holding the mallet was challenging enough. Successfully connecting the mallet with the ball absorbed all her focus and energy. They played for an hour and with each minute that passed Lani's appreciation for Asher's talent grew.

"I won't be able walk tomorrow," she groaned, the overworked muscles of her inner thighs protesting as she mounted the stairs to his apartment.

"You just need a hot bath and a massage." His eyes kindled. "I can help with both."

Lani emerged from the bedroom, dressed for work, jeans, boots, white button-down shirt and black leather jacket. Asher sat at the breakfast bar, a mug of coffee within easy reach as he texted. She wondered if his sister had responded to any of his messages. He'd reached out to her once a day since being released.

In the seconds before he noticed her arrival, she snatched the opportunity to regard him. Worn jeans hugged his lower half while a blue polo shirt molded to the muscles of his shoulders and chest. The faint scent of hay and horse hung in the air. He sat perched on a barstool, the heel of his left boot caught on the lower rung. He looked ready to spring into action. All this inactivity was clearly driving him crazy. He hummed like a live wire, his energy zapping and sizzling with the need to go and do.

She didn't know if she made a sound or if he was just so tuned in to her presence that he became aware he was no longer alone in the room. His eyes lifted from the phone screen and darted her way. The impact of his gaze raised goose bumps on her arms. A familiar breathless state came over her. This was bad. She never should've started up things with him again, but he was irresistible and she was powerless against her own longing.

"Have you heard back from Gina?" she asked, needing a distraction from her thoughts.

"Yeah." His neutral tone gave away none of his feelings. "She knows if anyone can find the money it will be you." His gaze roved ever so slowly over her outfit. "Looks like you're dressed for business. I guess we're not going to spend the morning in bed."

"You're the one who got up."

Her response was a little too tart. But honest all the same. Because deep down she was disappointed that he'd left her in bed to go tend to his horses. It had always been that way with her. She'd been so starved for his attention that any distraction left her feeling bereft and insecure.

"I didn't realize…" He set down his phone, held out his hand, a silent command to come to him and one she lacked the strength to ignore.

All too aware that a week earlier she might have flung up some sort of defense against him, Lani let herself be drawn toward him, nearly purring as his long fingers stroked her cheek and tangled in her hair. Her whole body swooned with pleasure as he hooked her hip with his other hand and drew her between his thighs. His lips grazed the sensitive skin below her ear and she shivered. Damn the man for being so good at this.

"You didn't realize what?"

There was a catch in her voice as she asked the question. He couldn't fail to hear it, couldn't fail to understand what caused it. When he touched her, she became someone else. Someone who forgot who she was, forgot right or wrong, up or down. There was just his touch anchoring her to him, helping her make sense of the emotional maelstrom inside her. All she needed was this man. His deep passionate kisses. His body possessing hers. The rest of the world didn't exist when he was kissing her.

"I didn't realize how much you miss me." He curved his hand over her butt and pulled her pelvis against the growing hardness behind his zipper. "When I'm not around."

Although it was true, confronting this chink in her armor was a puff of icy air against her hot skin. She stopped clinging to his impressive biceps and shoved against his chest. Not hard, nor with any vigor, but with enough pressure to part them, allowing her to take a half step back.

"I have a meeting in half an hour that I need to get to," she said, refusing to notice the smug light in his eye.

"May I come?"

Lani tugged her jacket straight, all too aware of the unfulfilled ache in her breasts and the clammy texture of her overheated skin. "Not a good idea."

"Because it's about the investigation?"

Plucking an elastic tie off her wrist, she fastened her hair into a low ponytail. "That *is* why I'm here."

"I hope that isn't the only reason why you are here."

He had her there. She'd already determined that he had no intention of skipping town. And the electronic bracelet around his ankle would allow the cops to track him down in a heartbeat if he ventured beyond the estate without her. She really didn't need to babysit him. In the beginning she'd stuck around to get inside his head. She could entertain the theory that he'd been set up and go back to her apartment in Dallas.

Yet the thought of being parted from him awoke a sharp pang of reluctance. She wasn't ready to move on from the long passionate nights in his arms. Or to ponder what might happen in the days to come.

"I really have to go," she said, uncomfortable with the direction her thoughts had gone.

"Who are you meeting?"

"Zach Benning."

The social media influencer had come to Royal to promote the festival and fallen in love with Lila Jones, Royal's Chamber of Commerce representative.

"I'd heard he's living in Royal now. Moved in with Lila Jones." Asher's gaze sharpened as it rested on her. "Gave up his entire life in LA just to be with her."

Lani found herself bristling at his thoughtful tone. What point was he trying to make? That she should've given up her plans for a master's degree five years earlier and trailed after him like some lovesick idiot? For how long? He'd offered her nothing she could count on. Made no promises. He had no plan for what they would do in Royal. She was a girl who needed a set of achievable goals to move her forward. Playing things by ear was *not* in her comfort zone.

"Yes, well…" She glanced toward the kitchen, dodging his assessing gaze. "I'd love a cup of coffee, but there's no time. I don't suppose you have a to-go mug?"

"I always have a to-go mug," he said, his lips lifting into a sardonic quirk. He was no stranger to their differences, but rather than ignore them, he was more likely to lean into the problems created between them.

"I'd really like it if you'd let me go along. Where are you meeting him?"

As he spoke, he went into the kitchen, pulled out a travel mug. Once he poured in the coffee and doctored it the way she liked, he handed it to her. Appreciation threatened as she took the mug. Damn him for being so good to her.

Against her better judgment, Lani felt herself softening toward his entreaty. Why not bring him along? He'd already proven a handy guy to have around and by sleeping with him she'd crossed a professional line. Plus, if she really believed that he wasn't responsible for taking the money, then maybe having his perspective would prove useful. Oh, hell. She was making excuses. Before this case she'd always worked alone and liked it. Relying on anyone besides herself meant she couldn't control the outcome.

"At the Royal Diner." She wondered if the public location would deter Asher.

He wasn't exactly anyone's favorite Edmond right now. A lot of people had suffered in town because of the failure of the festival. Keeping a low profile was a better way for him to go; but one thing about Asher, he never seemed to take the safest route.

"Will you wait while I change? I just need to get out of these barn clothes."

With a reluctant sigh, she nodded. "I'll call the monitoring company and let them know you're coming with me."

He winked at her before departing for the bedroom. Lani's insides turned to mush as her gaze locked on his tight rear end. A sigh whispered out of her before she realized what she was doing. *Stop!* Sure, the man had a body to die for and a knack for getting beneath her skin with his cocky smiles and heated glances, but she shouldn't indulge in his candy-coated yumminess during the day. She was a professional with a job to do. She needed to stay focused on that.

Before she'd finished her phone call, Asher had reappeared in clean denim and a light gray button-down shirt with the collar open to reveal the strong column of his throat. Her gaze locked on his tan skin as she remembered nibbling her way along it the night before and the heady sounds of his groans. She'd been so entranced by the sounds he'd made that she'd continued exploring him with her lips, teeth and tongue far into the night. A familiar flutter of excitement awakened deep in her belly as she picked up her laptop case.

"Let's get going," she said tersely, hating the husky note in her voice and the heavy pulse of longing that made her want to tear off his shirt and taste him once more.

"After you," he murmured, a wry smile softening his hard masculine features into irresistible boyish charm.

Did he know what she was thinking? She was known for her poker face, but he had a knack for reading her emotions. As they walked down the stairs toward the barn, she surreptitiously touched the back of her hand against her cheek. Was she warmer than normal? Did a hot pink flush betray the heat rising in her? How could she remain professional when her body betrayed her at every turn?

"Do you want me to drive?" he asked as their feet crunched along the gravel path, leading from the back of the barn to a series of turnout paddocks. Asher gestured to their cars, sitting side-by-side.

"No, I will."

"Okay." He sounded disappointed.

Lani shot him an impatient glance. "What?"

"I thought maybe after last night…" The previous evening they'd discussed her need to be in charge all the time.

"When it comes to my case, what I say goes."

"Yes, boss." He coupled his snarky comeback with a long-suffering sigh.

"I'm not your boss."

His raised eyebrows said she was sure acting like one.

"You like being in control. It seems like having a minion would suit you." He shot her a wicked grin before heading toward the passenger side of her SUV.

He was right. She wanted staff. More investigators meant she could take on more clients, but she needed more cases to be able to afford to hire anyone. When she'd started her investigative business, she hadn't taken into consideration how important contacts would be. Which was why solving this case for Kingston Blue was so critical. Finding the missing festival funds and bringing the embezzler to justice would boost her reputation.

Which was why it made no sense that with so much riding on this case, she was sleeping with the one man who everyone thought was guilty.

"If driving is that important to you," she snapped, deflecting her self-reproach onto him, "then be my guest."

"Thanks."

This single word, spoken with gratitude and delight,

further inflamed her heated emotions. All he was trying to do was be helpful. He wanted to participate in clearing his name and she continued to behave like a prickly pear cactus. It wasn't his fault that she'd made the mistake of crossing the professional line. She could've been stronger. Punishing him for her transgression wasn't fair.

Stewing, Lani slid into the passenger seat of his luxury sedan and tried not to enjoy the way she sank into the butter-soft leather.

"So how come you're meeting with Zach?" Asher asked as they sped through the estate gates and turned onto the highway. "Do you think he could be guilty?"

"I'm talking to everyone involved with the festival. And no, I don't think he's guilty. For one thing, he has a lot of money already."

"Yes, but he makes that money as a social media influencer. Something he's put on hold since moving to Royal. Maybe it was embezzling funds from the festival that gave him the ability to leave his life as an influencer behind."

Lani wasn't sure if she was more surprised by the fact that Asher had obviously been doing some research of his own regarding the festival's participants or the theories he'd developed for why Zach might be a suspect. She'd never given him credit for being capable of such serious, deliberate thought. And that certainly wasn't fair. Yet had he ever indicated that his thoughts were full of anything other than where the next party or exhilarating adventure was?

She winced. How often had she noticed that there was more to Asher than met the eye and then dismissed it as ridiculous? Had it been fair to look no deeper than his gorgeous appearance and his party-boy antics and assume that was all he had to offer? Five years earlier he'd given her a taste of his luxury lifestyle and she'd assumed because he hadn't earned his money that she was better than him.

Is that why she'd determined from the start that it would be a summer fling and nothing more? Because she didn't believe he wasn't capable of or interested in being more than that? She'd avoided discussing serious matters with him. Was that to keep from dwelling on his shallowness or dodge getting too attached? When she'd confessed her love to him, what had she expected would happen between them? Despite toying with the idea of not going on to grad school, the thought of altering her meticulous plans for the future had unnerved her.

Or had she done him a disservice? He hadn't seemed to mind their casual interaction. Lani thought about those true crime books sitting on his shelf. Had getting to know her that summer sparked a passion for unsolved murders? He'd asked a lot of questions about her process and thrown himself into helping her find the missing money. Would he be as interested if he hadn't been charged with the crime?

How come you haven't taken on any associates?

Was that just idle curiosity or was there something more behind the question?

Lani glanced at his profile and wondered what it would be like to partner with someone. To have another person to talk to about cases. To brainstorm ideas. To interact with clients.

No. She'd be crazy to even consider letting Asher get

anywhere near her business. She was doing just fine on her own. She'd be doing better after the successful conclusion of this case. After that, she'd go her way and Asher would go his. It was what had happened before. It would happen this time too.

Eight

A merry bell sounded as Asher pulled open Royal Diner's front door. Both a welcome and a warning, the tinkle seemed louder than usual because the classic diner-style restaurant was only half-full. Asher braced as his shocking appearance stirred the atmosphere. For the last week or so he'd actually forgotten about his increased notoriety around town. But now, as the whispers began, Asher ground his molars. He wasn't used to so much negativity directed his way.

Twenty feet of black-and-white-checkerboard tile separated them from the red vinyl booth where Zach Benning sat. A dozen pairs of unfriendly eyes watched his progress as Asher followed Lani past the counter service area. Curiosity and contempt battered him, but he acted oblivious to the commotion he was causing.

Asher focused his attention on the guy they'd come

to meet. His gray designer T-shirt gave him an LA vibe. Coupled with his expensive haircut, Zach looked every inch a city boy.

"Hi, Zach, thanks for meeting me." Lani glanced Asher's way before amending, "Meeting with *us*."

"Sure." Zach's eyebrows sank below the rim of his sunglasses as Asher slid into the red vinyl booth beside Lani. "You're out?" This he directed at Asher.

"On bail." Lani spoke up before Asher could explain and her quick explanation left him feeling defensive.

Retreating into sardonic humor, he stuck out his leg and showed off the edge of the ankle monitor. "I'm on a short leash."

This seemed to mollify the other man because after scrutinizing the device, he gave a short, satisfied nod, dismissing Asher as a threat. After that, Zach focused his full attention on Lani and the volume rose on his charisma as he pointed a lopsided smile in her direction. Asher bristled as Lani relaxed beside him.

The two men were close in age and similar in nature, each preferring a freewheeling lifestyle of parties, women and luxury. But where Asher was cavalier about his image, Zach had cultivated his particular bad-boy style into a huge social media following that had made him a multi-millionaire.

Familiar with Lani's weakness for pleasure-seeking reprobates, Asher slung an arm across the back of the booth behind her shoulders and twisted his upper body so he could easily watch the pair interact.

"As I mentioned on the phone, I'm looking into the money that's gone missing from the festival."

Zach's gaze flicked toward Asher and the corners of

his lips flattened in derision. "Shouldn't you be asking this guy?" He kicked his thumb in Asher's direction.

"I didn't take the money," Asher growled, letting his annoyance get the better of him. "I'm trying to figure out who did."

"You're trying to figure out…?" Zach looked from Asher to Lani. "I thought you were the one doing the investigating."

Lani gave Asher's thigh a hard nudge with her knee in warning and leaned forward, resting her forearms on the table. "I'm exploring the possibility that someone set Asher up."

While it wasn't a resounding declaration of confidence in his innocence, the tight knot of irritation eased in his chest. Most days he vacillated between relief that she was finally looking into alternate theories of the theft and worry that, without any evidence pointing to another's guilt, her logical mind would return to the most obvious theory that he was responsible.

"Somebody?" Zach echoed. "Like who?"

"Various people." She paused. "I'm talking to anyone who had a connection to the festival—"

"Wait one second," Zach interrupted vehemently, leaning forward. "I had nothing to do with the actual operations and—"

Lani threw up her hands in a pacifying gesture. "Not you, of course." She softened her expression, but didn't actually smile.

"If you're going after Lila, I've got nothing more to say."

"No. No. It's nothing like that," Lani assured him.

Lila Jones was a member of the festival's advisory

board in addition to working for the Royal Chamber of Commerce. A hardworking, serious-minded woman, rather forgettable in Asher's book, she'd engaged Zach to promote the festival through social media. Apparently seeing potential where no one else had, Zach had sprinkled some sort of fairy godmother dust on her and turned Lila into an Instagram sensation. The pair had become romantically involved and Lila had been seen around town sporting an enormous diamond on her left hand.

Although normally Asher paid little attention to the love lives of those around him, he was beginning to see a pattern of couples finding each other thanks to the ill-fated festival. He glanced Lani's way. Would that same magic work for them?

"But you were around many who were involved," Lani continued, "and I wanted to hear your impressions."

"I don't know how I can help you." Zach's tension eased marginally. "Early on I showed up, did a photo shoot—not anywhere near the actual site of the festival because of all the construction for the stages and restaurants. I didn't meet all that many people."

Lani offered an encouraging smile. "I'll bet you know more than you realize."

"It was all pretty chaotic. Really disorganized." Zach looked thoughtful. "Wait. Now that I think back, I did catch wind of how materials weren't showing up because bills weren't getting paid. Money problems were delaying everything." Once again Zach glanced toward the guy who everybody thought was the guilty party.

Asher's gut tightened. He could almost hear Lani's

brain whirring as she processed what Zach had to say. Okay, so obviously something fishy had been going on with the money all along. And yeah, he should've paid more attention, but the day-to-day details of the project had really not been his cup of tea.

"Besides the funding, did anything else strike you as unusual or wrong?"

"Not really." But Zach grew thoughtful. "Well, maybe this one thing. I kept seeing a guy that I thought I knew from back in LA."

Beside him, Lani stiffened, but her voice sounded nonchalant, almost blasé as she asked, "What guy?"

"Your brother's friend," Zach directed this remark to Asher. "I can't remember the name he introduced himself as, but I remember running into him several times in LA. The names didn't match. But I *swear* it was the same guy."

Ross's friend? Asher thought back to everyone who'd been to the island. When they were pitching it to various vendors and people they knew, they'd brought hordes of people to check out the site and hear the pitch. That had been the fun part… Entertaining the investors, painting a picture of the exclusive event, the delicious food, fantastic wine, the famous headliners like Kingston Blue set to perform, with all the proceeds going to charity.

Turns out he'd done too good a sell. In fact he'd oversold the festival. *Literally.*

The festival had suffered from neglect on the part of the principal players. Ross had been focused on his reunion with Charlotte and getting to know his two-year-old son, Ben. His attention was further disrupted by the major blowup this had caused with Rusty. Being disinherited can sure distract a guy. Sort of like being falsely accused of embezzlement.

Gina had been preoccupied with her mother's return to Royal after a nineteen-year absence and the family drama that had ensued.

That left Asher. His talents involved persuading people to trust him and painting their investors a picture of how awesome the festival was going to be. Initially he'd brought in a lot of the funds that had then gone missing.

"Which friend is that?" Lani asked, returning Asher's attention to the conversation. "Can you describe him?"

"Tall guy. Dark hair. Blue eyes. He seemed as if he knew the family really well. And he spent a lot of time sucking up to your dad."

It sounded like Billy Holmes. Ross's friend from college. He'd been a major player in the festival organization and always seemed to be around.

"You said you couldn't remember his name," Lani began, but before she could go much further into the questioning, Zach snapped his fingers and cut her off.

"Howard Bond," he declared. "No wait, not Howard Bond…"

While Zach scrunched up his face and racked his memory, Asher struggled to keep from shouting at the guy to get on with it. What the hell was going on? Who was Howard Bond? And what did any of this have to do with the embezzled money?

"Bond Howard," Zach announced, looking pleased. "That's it. I remember meeting the guy at a pool party thrown by an executive producer at Universal. I usually meet a lot of people at these events, but he stuck out in my mind as being a first-class dick."

"Why was that?" Lani asked, her flat tone hinting at only casual interest while Asher's heart thumped like a pile driver at the unexpected direction this interview was going.

"The party was loud and I didn't catch his name at first so he repeated it. He's all like, *it's Bond, as in James Bond.*" Zach intoned this like an exaggerated imitation of Sean Connery. "I thought to myself, that's crazy because who names their kid Bond? More likely he was called Howard and his last name is Bond so because it was LA, and everybody changes their name, he switched it to Bond Howard, which is much cooler."

While Zach was telling this tale, Asher noticed that Lani's body had begun to hum with excitement. She was like a bloodhound on a scent and it totally turned him on.

"So, when I met him on the island, and he was introduced as something else, it struck me as odd. Especially when he insisted we'd never met."

Lani narrowed her eyes. "Did you doubt it was the same person?"

"No, I was pretty sure it was the same guy. He has a fairly distinctive look. Do you know what I mean? Not like you'd mistake him for a bunch of other people."

Was this a legit lead? Asher glanced at Lani, but her expression remained inscrutable. He wanted to end this meeting with Zach and get her alone so he could figure out what was going on in that big beautiful brain of hers. Hope was tapping on the edge of his consciousness, wanting in. For the first time since his whole world

came crashing down around him, Asher realized the
level of fear he been suppressing. His hands began to
shake as the truth of his reality struck him. In the back
of his mind, he'd been grappling with going to jail for a
crime he hadn't committed. Only now, as it was looking
like someone else might be a suspect, did traction set in.

"Well that sounds promising," Asher said, keeping
a lid on his excitement as they stood up and headed toward the exit of the Royal Diner.

Before they reached the exit, the chime above the
door rang, warning him someone was coming in. Both
he and Lani slowed to let the new arrival enter. Deputy
Vesta entered, tipping his hat to Lani as she headed out
past him. Asher started to follow, but found the deputy in his way. Before he could step aside, Vesta had
bumped his broad shoulder hard into Asher's chest as
he went by. Although the blow didn't throw him off
balance, the hit jolted his ego, reminding him that in
the eyes of the town, he was a thief who'd stolen from
people who couldn't afford the losses.

In a much more subdued frame of mind, Asher
lengthened his stride to catch up with Lani. "Why do
you think Billy would've introduced himself as Bond
Howard?" he asked, picking up their earlier conversa-
tional thread.

"First of all, we're not really sure if this Bond Howard and Billy Holmes are the same person."

Asher appreciated Lani's caution about as much as
a pie in the face. He wanted her to leap all over this
lead and chase it down to prove she believed in his innocence and would go to any lengths to exonerate him.

Instead, she showed every sign of proceeding with her plodding, methodical investigation.

"How do we go about figuring out if they are?" Asher asked, letting just a bit of his impatience show.

He unlocked his car and swung the passenger door open for Lani. She shot him the oddest look before sliding into the car.

"What?" he prodded.

"I can open my own doors."

"Stop being so damned independent," he growled, wishing she understood how much he enjoyed taking care of her. "Let me help once in a while."

Asher wasn't just talking about the car door. He wanted to impress upon her that he was someone she could rely on. She might be too proud to accept financial help from him, but he could be there for her in other ways. As a sounding board to bounce ideas off of. As muscle in case she got into another tight situation like the one with Mika Sorenson's husband.

"Whatever."

She pulled the door shut, leaving him standing on the sidewalk, staring at her through the side window. How could this woman be so sensual and yielding in bed and stubborn and prickly out of it? Naked in his arms, she gave every part of herself to the moment and to him. But heaven forbid he fixed her favorite cocktail or made her dinner or—*gasp*—opened her car door, because then she became surly and churlish.

By the time he circled the car and slipped behind the wheel, she had her laptop out and was madly clicking away on the keys. From her extreme focus he might as well not have been in the car at all.

"Where to?" he asked, starting the engine. If it had been up to him, he would've driven straight to Billy Holmes's house and demanded answers.

"Just a second."

Asher was growing accustomed to Lani's ability to block out all distractions when she was investigating and didn't take offense when she put him off.

Still, he decided to do some musing out loud. "Why do you suppose Billy was using a different name in LA?"

"We don't know that it was Billy."

"But Zach seemed pretty sure," Asher argued. "And he was right about Billy's look being distinctive."

Lani made some noncommittal noises and continued to work away at her laptop. With a weary sigh, he put the car in gear, signaled and pulled out of the parking spot. One way to find out about Billy was to ask the guy himself. A tempting move, but he suspected he would do himself no favors if he started confronting people and accusing them of the theft. However he could go ask the suspect's good friend, Asher's brother, Ross.

They were halfway to The Edmond Organization when Lani looked up from her laptop and realized they weren't on their way back to the estate. "Where are we going?"

"To talk to Ross. He's known Billy since college and they've kept in touch all these years. Surely he knows what his good friend has been up before he moved to Royal two years ago."

"Are you out of your mind?" She rolled her eyes. "We can't barge into Ross's office and start asking a bunch of invasive questions about his friend."

"Why not?"

When she didn't immediately answer, Asher glanced her way. Her pained expression was like a knife in his chest.

"Why the hell not, Lani?" he demanded, a sick feeling swirling through him.

"A few months back your brother was struggling financially."

"You don't seriously think that Ross was involved in this embezzlement, do you?"

He couldn't believe what he was hearing. Ross wouldn't do something like that to him. Yet even as he rejected Lani's inference, her logic began eroding his trust. Whom was he supposed to put his faith in? The man he'd called brother since he was a teenager? Or the woman he'd spent a fun-filled summer frolicking with? The same one who was currently investigating him for embezzlement?

"Let's put it this way, I suspect everyone." Her answer was a sharp kick that connected with his head and set his temples to throbbing.

"Including me," he stated flatly, gripping the steering wheel until his knuckles turned white.

"Yes."

Presuming he'd made inroads with her had been too optimistic. Just because they were sleeping together, didn't mean her opinion of him had improved. No. Just as it had been between them five years ago, he was little more than a walk on the wild side for her. She'd been clear from the start that she couldn't take him seriously. He wasn't relationship material.

While he'd been ruminating, she'd gone back to typing. If they weren't heading to the Edmond headquarters, he needed some destination. "So, where are we going?"

If Lani heard the tension in his voice, she made no sign. "I think the best thing is to head back to Elegance Ranch. I have some research to do on this Bond Howard character. We need to figure out if he and Billy are the same guy."

"And how do we do that?"

"Well, we can start with his social media."

"Billy's?" Asher had no idea how that was supposed to help.

Lani shook her head. "Bond Howard's."

Asher gave her space to work as he drove back to the estate. The moments of freedom he'd known while driving during his all-too-brief trip to the Royal Diner left him hyperaware of how little he'd appreciated his freedom until now.

As the estate gates loomed, he had a fleeting but overwhelming urge to turn the car around and head straight for the airport. He knew he wouldn't get anywhere with the electronic-monitoring device strapped to his ankle, but a jittery restlessness had taken hold of him. In the past he had exorcized his demons by indulging in some sort of risky action. That door was shut and barred to him for now. He would just have to face his reality and learn to make the best of it.

The thought actually made him grin. Was this what personal growth was all about? It figured it would take something as drastic as looming imprisonment to wake him up.

"Any luck finding Bond Howard's social media presence?" he asked as the car raced past the main house and made for the stable.

"Hmm."

It really was time for a change, he mused. As much as he enjoyed living close to his horses, he really should put the entire string up for sale and move away from Elegance Ranch.

"There's quite a bit actually," Lani said, clicking away on her laptop. "Turns out he has several online personas."

Asher mulled that bit of news as he parked beside her SUV. Her preoccupation with whatever data she was finding gave him enough time to shut off the car, exit and have her door open before she closed the lid. He smirked at her scowl and went the extra mile by offering his hand to help her out of the low-slung sedan.

The tingle in his fingers shot straight to his groin. He pushed all thoughts of sex from his brain and asked, "How did you find the additional social media profiles so quickly?"

"I have software that allows me to find similar images on the internet. Already the search has yielded profiles for Bobby Hammond and Brad Howell, in addition to Bond Howard."

"That looks pretty suspicious," Asher said, hoping she agreed.

"Maybe." She started for the stairs to the apartment. "We'll need to do some more digging before that becomes clear."

"We'll," he echoed, grinning. "I like the sound of that."

Nine

For days after their meeting with Zach, Lani kicked herself for letting Asher think he was participating in the investigation. It was hers to handle. She shouldn't have involved him at all. And the excuse that she enjoyed his company was too lame for her to acknowledge even though it was absolutely the case. So much for her lone-wolf policy. Maybe she'd been too quick to downplay her need for associates. His determined approach to the task was altering her attitude. Sure, his style was different from hers. But that didn't mean his results weren't sound. Could she let go of her need to control the entire process? *Should* she?

Still, day after day they'd set up their laptops at his breakfast bar. Side by side, typing away in companionable silence. She'd done a deep dive into Bond Howard while Asher researched Bobby Hammond and Brad

Howell. Sure enough, Billy Holmes had been living in various parts of the country under different names. They'd contacted anyone who had tagged him in their photos and a picture was beginning to form. The women were quickest to respond. Asher and Lani discovered Billy had left a trail of jilted lovers and unsatisfied investors in his wake. Everyone was angry.

And now he was comfortably ensconced in the Edmond estate, living rent-free in one of the guesthouses and showing no sign of moving on. Lani gazed in the direction of the main house, wondering how a college friendship had translated into the relationship Billy now enjoyed with the entire Edmond family. From what she could tell, he was practically a member of the family. Did Ross know about Billy's multiple identities? She hadn't seen the two men interacting. Was it possible that they'd been working together to bring the festival down?

If so…why?

It was well-known that once Ross's former lover—and their child that she'd never told him about—had returned to town, his relationship with his father had completely fallen apart to the point where Rusty had disinherited his biological son. Would Ross's financial troubles have made him an unwitting pawn in Billy's schemes? Or had Ross gotten in over his head and chosen to frame his own brother for the crime to avoid taking the fall?

Either way they couldn't tip off either man until she gathered more information.

"It's not looking too good for our boy, is it?" Asher's delight broke through Lani's introspection. His lopsided smile had appeared. For the first time since she'd visited him in jail, he looked genuinely relieved.

Although she wanted to reassure him, her instincts warned her to be cautious. "Not at all."

Asher's good mood dimmed. "You don't sound all that sure."

"It looks bad," Lani agreed. "But nothing we've turned up is proof that Billy is connected to anything illegal with the Soiree on the Bay festival. Adopting multiple aliases and convincing wealthy women to invest in his business ideas might be sketchy, but not every venture is successful. Maybe the guy is better at ideas than execution."

"So I'm still the bad guy."

He'd raked his fingers through his hair frequently over the course of the last two hours and several unruly spikes poked up in various directions. She liked his disheveled look. It reminded her of all those mornings when she'd awoken in his bed and watched him sleep. She'd known such joy in those unguarded moments. Anything had seemed possible. Like she could have it all... The satisfying career she craved. A happy life with the man who showed her how to let go and have fun. Lani pushed away the fantasy. These dreams of the perfect future were a distraction she couldn't afford.

"Look, don't give up hope." She set her hand on his shoulder and squeezed. "We'll find something."

Asher took both her hands in his and faced her. His somber expression made her stomach drop. She traced his features with her gaze, absorbing the sensual curve of his lips, the strong bones of his face, the hint of stubble that blurred the sharp jut of his jaw. Naked emotion flickered in his dark brown eyes. Relief. Gratitude. And something…*more*. Her breath caught at the vulnerability she glimpsed in that unguarded moment. She set her palm on his chest. In the stillness that followed, her heart found a new rhythm and beat in sync with his.

A second later he lowered his thick lashes and the link between them snapped. The recoil stung. Neither one of them was brave enough to acknowledge the connection between them for long. Yet each day it grew stronger. The ache more acute when they were apart. And unlike when they'd been together that summer, she was losing the will to resist her longing to be with him. In the sensible moments when her emotions weren't in control, she wondered what would happen when this case ended.

"I hope you realize how much I appreciate that you believe in me," Asher said, covering her hand on his chest and giving a light squeeze. "I don't know how I would've gotten through this without you."

Lani's throat tightened, making speech impossible. This would be the perfect moment to tell him that she still had doubts about his innocence. Her last report to Kingston Blue had been objective and scrupulously professional. Afraid that she was letting her personal feelings interfere with her judgment, she hadn't voiced her suspicions that Asher might have been set up. Once again she had prioritized her career over her personal life and doubted Asher would understand.

Instead of facing her mistakes, she apologized to him in a way that they could both appreciate.

"Hey," she murmured, sliding her fingers through

his hair and offering him her best come-hither smile. "I could use a snack."

Asher's sleepy gaze stroked her features. "I'm feeling a little hungry myself."

"You know I'm not talking about food, right?"

His wicked grin said it all. "What did you have in mind?"

She slid off the stool and snagged his waistband, drawing him toward the living room. "It's about time we christen this chair, don't you think?"

"Oh, yes. I'd been thinking that exact thing just an hour ago."

"And you didn't bring it up?" she teased, unfastening his belt, the button on his jeans and the zipper below. With her breath escaping her lungs on a languid sigh, she burrowed under all the fabric and dropped to her knees before him, taking his clothes with her. At her urging, he stepped out of each pant leg, letting her undress him. His fingers brushed a stray lock off her cheek. She knew he would tangle his hands in her hair later, riding the movement of her head as she brought him pleasure with her mouth.

Lani placed her hands on his thighs, palms skimming his hair-roughened skin, past his jutting erection and over the smooth, chiseled plains of his abdomen. There, she gave a gentle shove and he sat down in the armchair with a quiet grunt of surprise. Then she was parting his knees and sliding between them. Her fingers began working the buttons of his shirt. When she had them undone, she spread the fabric wide and leaned forward to press a kiss to his throat. His Adam's apple worked as he swallowed hard and she smiled as she nipped and nuzzled her way to his ear, across his jaw and finally to the corner of his mouth. He turned and slanted his head so their lips met. Their open-mouth kiss was a slow, sultry tease of breath and flicking tongue. Lani's hands tracked down his chest and stomach, savoring the splendid muscle beneath all his silken skin. The man was perfection in so many ways.

With her hot gaze on his arousal, she set to peeling off her own clothes. Stripped down to her underwear, she fondled her breasts through her lace bra before bracing her hands on the chair's arms and bending forward.

"Care to do the honors?"

"My pleasure."

He reached behind her and popped the bra clasp. The fabric fell into his grasp and she bestowed a saucy wink.

"Thank you."

As the ache between her thighs intensified, Lani skimmed her palm down her belly and beneath the edge of her panties. Because he loved to watch her like this, she threw her head back, rolled her hips from side to side and pressed her fingertips against her clit. Wetness soaked her panties. When he made a strangled sound, she opened her eyes and focused on his face.

A moment later she dropped to her knees once more and let her hair down, knowing he adored the seductive slide of the strands against his skin. With a brazen smile, she moved between his thighs and wrapped her fingers around his erection without warning or preliminaries. A breath ejected from his lungs, a startled curse that made her smile.

Lani eased her hold on his shaft. "Too much?"

"No." The single syllable wheezed out of him as her

thumb circled the head of his shaft, sliding over the bead of moisture she found there before gliding her fingers to the base. "It's perfect."

Asher clenched his fingers over the chair's arms and settled deeper into the seat, offering his body for her to play with. She repeated the stroking motion, watching the way his head dropped back and his lips parted. He watched her from beneath heavy lidded eyes, tiny flecks of copper blazing in their depths. While his posture looked relaxed, his expression remained tight with anticipation. She understood. She couldn't wait to get her mouth on him. And why bother holding back when that's what he wanted too?

She licked her lips and lowered them over his blunt head, purring in delight at the salty taste of the velvety flesh. A growl tore from Asher's throat as she flicked her tongue over him, tormenting him the way he had done to her the night before.

"God, Lani."

Her name on his lips was heaven. She decided to reward him. Shutting her eyes to block out all distraction, she hummed and took him in, the vibration making him jerk in reaction. He was clutching the arms of the chair now, bracing to endure the wicked pleasure she was giving him.

Making her lips into a tight circle, she took as much as him into her mouth as she could handle. It was a lot, but she'd learned how to relax and open for him. When the head of his erection hit the back of her throat, his fingers slipped into her hair. He played with the strands, applying no pressure as she withdrew, circled him with her tongue and bobbed backed down again.

His appreciative murmur, punctuated with the occasional hiss of acute pleasure were the only sounds that came from him. He'd let her know when he was close. Communicate if he wanted her to finish him in this way or climb aboard. In the meantime she would make this a night to remember. By alternating between teasing and deep dives, she held him on the brink longer than she expected.

But his willpower was only so resilient and she'd mastered the art of pleasuring him this way. When he cupped her face in his hands and angled her head away from his erection, her body awakened with delight. He covered her swollen lips in a tender kiss that tangled their tongues and said without words how deeply he appreciated her.

"Come here."

He pulled her up off the floor and drew her onto the chair. There was just enough room for her knees on either side of his hips. His long fingers bracketed her hips, moving her into position. His thick shaft bobbed against her thigh, seeking the connection they both hungered for.

Lani gasped as he speared into her dripping heat. Utterly turned on, the full length of him filling her was nearly enough to trigger her orgasm. She was close… so close. Swollen with longing and impatient with need, when his mouth closed over the tip of one breast and sucked hard, she knew there would be no more holding back. Her hips bucked enthusiastically against him, grinding her clit against his pelvic bone, and a heartbeat later, her climax ripped through her.

She clutched his head against her breast, riding him

hard, launched even higher at the scrape of his teeth against her nipple. The bliss seemed to go on and on, aided by the length of him driving into her over and over. Lani gasped and cried out, ridiculous incoherent chanting as her pleasure soared higher, so much higher. She could scarcely breathe. Surely she should have plateaued by now. But his persistent thrusts, so smooth and with perfect rhythm, made her muscles tense and coil as she ascended toward the peak of yet another orgasm. He'd done this for her before. Made her come and come and come again.

It's what made her crazy for him. His body, his soul, the heart he tried to protect. He was the one she'd dreamed about before they'd ever met and long after they'd parted. Fate had brought them back together. Now it was up to them to figure out how to make it work. Because this time she didn't want to say goodbye.

Had it only been three weeks since he'd been arrested for embezzling the festival funds? It felt like the threat of imprisonment had been hanging over him for far longer. How ironic that the worst thing that had ever happened to him resulted in something as wonderful as bringing Lani Li back into his life.

The last week together had been nothing short of magic. They'd returned to the playful camaraderie and sizzling passion of five years earlier. There were moments when he was convinced everything would turn out okay, but then he'd bump the electronic monitor on his ankle and the whole miserable mess returned to his awareness in a hurry.

Asher shook hands with the horse trainer who'd ar

rived to pick up Royal Flush. As they loaded her into the trailer for the journey to California, he walked away with a tight throat and a heart ready for fresh opportunities,

The money he'd gotten for Royal Flush would clear the debt between him and Lani. Sacrificing his favorite mount demonstrated his willingness to grow. As much as he'd loved them, the horses tied him to his old life. They had been his comfort when his relationship with Rusty floundered and offered direction when it came to his life's purpose.

Lani had been right to call him out all those years ago. He *had* been a directionless frat boy. But that had changed once he'd met her. And now that she was back in his life, he intended to evolve even more. New challenges awaited him and Lani was the key to what he wanted to do next.

Smiling, Asher attacked the stairs to his apartment, taking the steps two at a time. He was eager to share his new vision with Lani and see her reaction. She agreed with his assessment that The Edmond Organization wasn't the place for him. Tonight he was taking her to dinner, a celebration of the positive changes he was making in his life since she'd come back into it.

He'd chosen Sheen, not only because the restaurant was known for its exceptional cuisine, but also for being run and staffed by all women of various ethnicities. Ross's fiancée, Charlotte Jarrett, had returned to Royal to oversee the kitchen and had quickly made the restaurant a Royal favorite.

Lani had headed back to Dallas that morning to meet with a potential client and planned to return by six o'clock. That left Asher an hour to shower and get ready for their date. The word sent an electric zap through him. With his nerve endings buzzing pleasantly, he headed into the bathroom and the large mirror over the double vanity reflected back his goofy grin. He rubbed his palm over his stubbled cheeks, noted the sparkle in his eyes and remarked at the transformation joy had wrought. Damn, he was *happy*. Even to the point where he could appreciate the pain-in-the-ass electronic monitor clamped to his ankle, being charged with embezzlement and wire fraud had brought Lani back into his life.

Half an hour later Asher emerged from his closet dressed for dinner and realized he was no longer alone in the apartment. A cell phone was ringing in the living room. Eager to show Lani how much he'd missed her, he was halfway across the bedroom when he heard her answer the call.

"Hello, Kingston."

Asher slowed his pace as the name registered. Kingston, as in Kingston Blue? An image of the famous singer popped into Asher's mind. Above-average height with an imposing frame and a handsome face framed by long dreadlocks, his open and friendly manner combined with a wide white smile had disarmed and enchanted everyone. But it was his keen brown eyes that had told the real story as his gaze had scrutinized the construction happening at the festival site on Appaloosa Island, assessing the pros and cons before agreeing to headline Soiree on the Bay.

What was he doing calling Lani?

"What's up?" While she came across as calm and professional, Asher detected a wary note.

Moving carefully, he took several steps toward the door leading into the living room, the better to hear the conversation, aware that by eavesdropping he was questioning if he could trust Lani. In a flash he realized he was once again prioritizing his needs first and in doing so causing damage to their fledgling relationship. How could he hope to form a solid connection with her when the first time his faith was tested, he chose to doubt.

"...progress report," came the deep rich masculine voice. Lani must have had him on speaker.

Progress report? What progress report? Asher recalled how she'd avoided answering every time he asked her who hired her to look into the missing money. Was Kingston Blue that client? The man hadn't made all his money with his music. He was a savvy businessman, as well. And obviously one determined to locate what had been stolen from him.

"As I mentioned before," Lani said, "this case is a lot more complicated than it seemed. The money vanished from the bank accounts right after the funds were transferred. The feds think the money was moved offshore, but there's no trace of those accounts on Asher's work or personal computers, his phone or in his house. If he was funneling the money away from the festival accounts, then he was very careful about it."

"If?" Concern deepened Kingston Blue's voice. "You disagree with the feds about Asher Edmond's guilt?"

"I know the evidence points to him. His name is on the house in the Maldives," she said, "and his online signature triggered the wire transfers. But he could've been set up."

A pregnant silence followed her words. Asher's heart hammered. While it sounded like she was defending him, this conversation drove home the fact that she'd ultimately come to Royal to find the missing festival funds. Something he'd conveniently put to the back of his mind.

"I hired you because of your previous relationship with Asher," Kingston Blue said. "I assumed you would use that connection to get information out of him about where the money ended up."

Kingston's words scored a direct hit. Asher set his hand on the wall as his thoughts reeled. All this time she'd been playing him for a fool. While he shouldn't be surprised, that didn't make the emotional blow less devastating. She made it very clear five years ago that her career came first and he was just a reckless playboy without a future. Well, one thing was true, obviously she'd gotten a lot better at acting.

"That's not how I work," Lani said stiffly. "I've been looking into various people involved in the festival and Asher isn't the only one with access to those funds. His brother Ross—"

Kingston Blue interrupted her. "It seems to me you're just offering me excuses why you think your ex-boyfriend is innocent. I'm not paying you to exonerate him."

"Asher was never my boyfriend." Her voice was stark and fervent on that point. "I'm not emotionally involved with him now if that's what you're thinking. You hired me to find the money and if you can be patient with me a little longer, that's what I intend to do."

"By chasing random leads."

"By doing a *thorough* investigation," Lani insisted. "As soon as investigators found the house in the Maldives, they stopped looking at anyone else."

"There's overwhelming evidence that Asher's the one who transferred the funds out of the festival account. Where they went is what I want to know."

"So do I," she said. "But I need to figure out who actually stole the money."

"Asher Edmond."

"Maybe." Lani sounded less than thrilled to be arguing with her client. "But I'm also looking into someone else. Billy Holmes."

"Who is that?"

"Friend of the family. He lives at the Edmonds' estate. I've discovered he has a suspicious background and I'd like to pursue the lead."

Kingston Blue paused before answering as if weighing his options. "You have three days. After that you're off the case."

Asher took several seconds to compose himself before emerging from the bedroom. Lani was standing by the large window that overlooked the extensive manicured grounds between the barn and the main house.

"You're back early," he remarked, crossing the room to pull her back against his body and place a kiss on her cheek. "How'd the meeting with the new client go?"

She stiffened momentarily before relaxing into his embrace. "Good. She hired me."

"Then we should celebrate." Asher headed into his

kitchen to pull a bottle of champagne from the wine cooler, and set two glasses on the breakfast bar. "You have a new client. I sold Royal Flush."

"You want to celebrate that?" Lani asked, drawing near. "That's been a big part of your life. I thought you'd be sad that she was gone."

Asher focused on pulling the cork from the bottle rather than look at her. He was still processing the call he'd overheard.

"It was hard to part with her, but she's too well trained to waste away here." Asher pictured the chest-nut tearing across the polo field and smiled. "And since her new owner paid me a hundred thousand dollars for her, I can pay you back the money you put up for my bail and compensate you for the time you spent on my case."

This last part he'd added to test her reaction.

"I already have a client." She looked uncomfortable. "You know that."

"Is there some reason you can't have two?"

"I'm not sure that your goals aren't in conflict."

"It seems as if everyone wants to find the money. Including me." He extended a glass filled with bright sparkling liquid toward her. "I'd also like to find out who stole it. I don't see how we could possibly be in conflict."

"I just don't think it's a good idea."

Dismayed by the fact that she continued to let him think that Rusty had hired her, Asher chose not to push any further. No doubt she had her reasons for keeping him in the dark. The fact that they were at odds as long as this case remained open was not the problem. He was more concerned what would happen once everything had been wrapped up.

He lightly clicked his crystal flute against hers before taking a sip. He watched her surreptitiously while appearing to savor the champagne. She looked more miserable than he'd ever seen her. Obviously guilt wasn't a comfortable weight on her shoulders.

"Now that I've officially closed the door on any chance of a comeback as a professional polo player—"

"Was that a possibility?" she interrupted, arching one dark eyebrow.

"Hush. I've been thinking what I want to do next."

Retreating into his frat-boy act was familiar and would serve him better than venting his frustration over the investigation's slow progress.

"Next?" She looked resigned as she asked, "What about your position at The Edmond Organization?"

"I promised Rusty that I'd stick with it for two years. My time is up and after spending these weeks with you, I realize I rather enjoyed investigative work and I think I have a knack for it."

She gave an odd snort and then began to cough vigorously as if the champagne had gone up her nose rather than down her throat. "I'm sorry?" she wheezed. "Didn't you go to work for the family business after Rusty threatened to cut you off? How are you going to support yourself?"

"By partnering with you."

"Partnering…?"

"You're not the only one who can dig up information on people. I checked you out and it turns out your business is in a bit of a slump. It could use someone like me to bring in more high-profile clients."

Lani was staring at him as if had sprouted a set of horns. "Let me get this straight, you want to go into business with me?"

"Why so surprised?" He ignored the negative sweep of her head. "We work well together."

"I think you like dabbling in my investigation because it's a distraction. But once this case is over and if you're exonerated—"

"If?" Her meaning went through him like a hot blade. Without her on his side, eager to prove his innocence, he could still go to jail. Even if the money was recovered.

She continued speaking as if he hadn't interrupted her. "I'm convinced you'll lose interest in the kind of work I do."

Asher needed no further proof of Lani's low expectations about him and the hit blew a big hole in what he thought was developing between them. This constant feeling of not being good enough because he'd made mistakes in the past was getting old. No wonder he'd preferred traveling around the world playing professional polo to sticking around and seeing nothing but disappointment and disapproval in his father's eyes.

"Are you really worried that it's the investigative work I'm going to lose interest in?" he countered, frustration making him strike out at the one person he wanted to make happy.

She shifted her weight backward, a slow recoil from his insinuation. "What else?"

"Or is this about us?"

Ten

Us?

Lani stiffened at the question and leveled her gaze at him. The answer was too fraught with uncertainty to answer. Was Asher romancing her for the sole purpose of using her to change careers? She'd been worried that he wanted her on his side to clear him of the embezzlement charges, but now it seemed he wanted to move in on her business, as well.

"Is there an *us*?" she asked, unsure where to draw the line between reality and fantasy.

"You tell me. Are we going to keep seeing each other once the case is over?"

She could barely acknowledge to herself how much she wanted their sexual connection to develop into deep romantic love much less share that with Asher. Long ago she'd confessed her feelings and he'd rejected them. She couldn't face that same crushing disappointment again.

Lani bit her lower lip and grappled with how to answer him. "I don't know." She wanted to, but once the prescribed proximity of the investigation ended, would Asher even be interested in a personal relationship anymore? His interest in her business seemed to confuse the situation. "You live here in Royal and I'm in Dallas…" It was an obvious dodge given how they'd broken up last time.

"Once you were open to a long-distance relationship," he reminded her.

"And you made it very clear that it wasn't your thing."

"What if I moved to Dallas?"

Hope barreled through her, but she shut it down. Was this about their relationship or a business partnership? Had she let herself be played?

"Are you serious about quitting The Edmond Organization?"

"It's not for me," he told her.

"What about your horse training?"

"I'm already in the process of selling the string." His gaze increased in intensity as he spoke. "I'd like to help you with your business, but it's more important that you want to take a chance on me."

"I tried that once." She could barely get the words out past the lump in her throat. "It didn't work out so well for me."

"So you're saying you can't trust me."

"I don't honestly know. All this is coming at me so suddenly and there's a lot of upheaval in your life right now. Who knows how you'll feel once the case is closed and things settle down." As much as she wanted to trust him with her heart, she'd been devastated last time.

"Don't make this about how I feel," he said, wariness entering his expression. "I want to know how you feel. What are we doing? Is it just casual sex or are we going to turn it into something real?"

"Something *real*?" She tried the phrase on for size, but couldn't find comfort in the fit. "I don't know."

Even though they'd reconnected physically, her resistance to baring her heart put a wall between them. A wall she was loathe to tear down. Sex was one thing—they had explosive chemistry and it was easy to lose herself in the magic of his touch. However, as long as the embezzlement charge hung over his head, he needed her help with the investigation. Once it was over, she would reconsider taking the risk of getting emotionally entangled with him. But for now she couldn't in good conscience commit to that.

"Because you're using me to close your case and make your client happy?"

"I'm *not* using you." That was true even if it had been her plan at the start. Once her old feelings had surfaced, she'd lost the battle with how much she wanted him. "But I really don't know if we can make it work."

"Sounds like you've made up your mind." He stared at her for a long time while a muscle jumped in his jaw. "So, I guess that means you're putting me in your rearview mirror once more."

"*I'm* the one putting *you* in the rearview mirror?" Was she hearing him right? "I recall that I wanted to try the long-distance thing and you thought that was too much of a commitment."

Asher's gaze intensified. "And so you called us done and walked away."

"You didn't give me a whole lot of choice. Basically, it was either give up on grad school and run off with you to Argentina or we were over." Her blood raged white-hot as unresolved resentment flared. A second later fear and panic kicked in. She was on the verge of losing him all over again. "You didn't want to do the long-distance thing."

"Okay, so maybe that was a mistake."

Maybe?

"Or maybe neither one of us was ready for a committed relationship" she said. "And so we did the best thing we could do for ourselves and broke up."

"It wasn't that cut and dry for me."

What did that mean? Lani sucked in a deep breath in an effort to calm her wildly fluctuating emotions. She hadn't expected the fledgling intimacy between her and Asher to be tested so soon.

"What do you want me to say?" *That you were my first love and I never got over you?*

"I want you to be honest with me about how you feel."

"Honest." Her chest heaved as she gulped in a big breath. "Okay, if you want the truth, the reason I don't think it's a good idea for us to become business partners or any other kind of partner is that I'm not sure I can count on you."

From the first she'd recognized that they approached situations completely differently. Where her personality was a bullet shot from a gun, a swift straight line from problem to solution, Asher was like air. A gentle breeze coming at her from one direction. Then moments later a gust of wind that smacked into her blind side, knocking her off her feet.

"You still see me as that irresponsible frat boy." Asher scowled. "That's not who I am and hasn't been for a long time."

Yet he couldn't stick with anything. Not polo. Not the job with The Edmond Organization. Not her.

"Really?" she challenged. "Look at the mess you're in because you didn't take your responsibilities with the festival seriously."

"You have no idea what I take seriously. Yes, I had access to the accounts…"

"And someone—probably Billy Holmes—was able to take advantage of that."

"But it could've been any of us. Gina. Ross. Even Rusty given how close the two of them are. He chose me for some reason I don't get."

Lani heard Asher's sweeping frustration, but couldn't summon the courage to comfort him. "Hopefully I can figure that out. I'm heading to Las Vegas to meet with his mother tomorrow."

But Asher wasn't going to be thrown off topic. "What would it take for me to prove you can count on me?"

She dug her fingertips into the back of her shoulder where stress was pinching the nerves and gave her whirling brain a moment to process everything that was coming at her.

"I really don't know."

"Well, at least be straight with me on one thing. Do you think I stole the money from the festival?"

"No." At least she could give him a clear, decisive answer on that score.

He gave her a tight smile. "Well, I guess that's something. And the money for my bail. Do I return the hundred thousand dollars to you?"

Lani went cold. The intensity of the question put a hard lump in the pit of her stomach. Was he shooting in the dark or had he overheard her conversation with Kingston? She'd been careless when she didn't realize he was in the apartment.

When she didn't answer right away, he continued, "Or should I wire it directly back to Kingston Blue?"

Damn. Now he knew she'd been deceiving him from the start. "You can give it to me. I'll get it back to him."

His eyes narrowed. "Can I trust you?"

Although she knew it was a big show to get under her skin, Lani stiffened. "Of course."

"I'm not so sure. Knowing how complicated our relationship is, you let me believe my father hired you. How could you let me think he was finally on my side?"

Lani dropped her eyes to the floor. "I shouldn't have done that."

"No," he agreed. "You think you understand how messed up things are between us, but it's worse than you know. It was a big deal for me to believe that he wanted to help me out."

"Why such a big deal now when he's supported you since the day he married your mother?"

A sardonic smile ghosted across his lips. "He supported me. But there were conditions tied to it. Conditions I had no idea about until three years ago." Asher's grim expression made Lani's heart sink.

It was becoming clear that she'd made a huge error in judgment. "What sort of conditions?"

"He and my mother had a little side agreement regarding her alimony. She agreed that since I turned eighteen, any money he gave me came out of the payments he owed her. And as part of the deal, she wasn't allowed to tell me anything about what was going on."

Lani gasped. "Why would he do that?"

"Because he's a miserable excuse for a human being. I don't know if he regretted formally adopting me or if he just wanted to mess with her. A couple years ago, I found out she was nearly bankrupt and I couldn't understand why. She finally broke down and confessed what had been going on. I confronted Rusty and he offered me a bargain. He would pay my mother everything he'd withheld if I agreed to sign a five-year contract with The Edmond Organization."

"Did you?"

Asher kept his gaze fixed on the windows that faced the main house. "As much as I wanted to help my mother, I knew I wouldn't survive five years working for Rusty. Instead, I got him to agree to let me work for him for two and a half years in exchange for fifty-percent of the money he'd spent on me. That, and what I had in investments was enough to get her out of trouble."

"Why didn't you tell me this before?" Lani asked, her heart aching for all he'd been through.

"Why should I?" He shook his head. "When you already had more than enough reasons not to trust me."

He was right. She'd failed to believe him at every turn. And each time she'd been wrong.

"So now you know. I didn't quit polo because I was afraid to be cut off. I didn't join The Edmond Organization because I was trying to win Rusty's approval, and I'm not leaving because I can't stick with anything. I haven't sold off my horses because I'm tired of training. And I don't want to become your business partner as some sort of lark."

Lani had no words that could undo the damage she'd caused by not believing in him. "I'm sorry." It became immediately obvious this was the wrong thing to say.

"Don't be. It's my problem, not yours." With his lips flattened into a thin line, he raked his fingers through his hair. "Look, I don't feel much like celebrating tonight and it sounds like you've got a trip to get ready for. If it's okay with you, I think we should skip dinner and call it a night."

"Okay. I understand…"

And while she stood with her heart a lead stone in her chest, Asher headed into the master bedroom and closed the door behind him.

The morning after his fight with Lani, Asher woke with a headache and a really bad idea.

It was time for a party.

Not that he had anything to celebrate or was in the mood to be social. Lani had let him believe that she was on his side and that he had a reason to dream of a better future with her a big part of it. Nothing he'd done in the last three weeks had convinced her to give him a chance. She still perceived him as someone frivolous and shallow, unable to consider anyone's welfare but his own. Had he really thought by letting her in on his bargain with Rusty that her outlook toward him would suddenly be transformed? He was so tired of fighting everyone's bad opinion of him, of having to prove himself to people he loved.

The realization hit him like a piano falling from a very tall crane.

Damn.

He loved her. He loved Lani Li.

She was the one he let get away. Now he knew she was also the woman he couldn't live without. The one person he longed to spend the rest of his life laughing and fighting and making love with. The certainty had been building for days. It had taken a huge relationship-ending blowout for the fog to clear from his brain.

Was it any wonder he wanted to act out, to wallow in self-sabotage, letting everyone believe he was the same directionless jerk he'd always been?

He thought back to five years ago when he and Lani had first met. What if he'd been more serious back then instead of letting frivolous pursuits distract him? He could've saved his mother financial headaches and achieved a high level of success in his field. Instead he'd fallen short of expectations and reinforced Rusty's disapproval.

At the time he hadn't realized how he'd given his power away. Not until Lani had come along and opened his eyes to hard work and focused goal setting had he been filled by an optimistic sense of his own worth. How different things might've been if he'd had someone in his corner sooner.

Someone who could've channeled his ability to charm people into positive avenues. Much of what had appealed to him with the Soiree on the Bay festival was the chance to benefit others. How ironic that instead of helping people out, the whole situation had destroyed numerous lives.

Being the guy that everyone hated had been a wake-up call. Using his money and position to benefit others would be so much better than selfishly squandering everything he'd gained. When his accounts were unfrozen, he intended to make changes in his life. He would invest in other people's dreams, focusing his resources, time and energy on helping people.

But that was his future. In the now, the one woman he needed to believe in him couldn't. The agony lancing through his heart pushed him toward self-destructive behaviors. The old Asher would lose himself in fun. And nothing said fun like a lively party with a large group of friends. Since he wasn't allowed to go anywhere without Lani, he would just have to bring the party here.

Since he doubted very many people would show up for his benefit, Asher reached out to Gina for help.

"Call everyone you know. We're throwing a party at Elegance Ranch."

"Are you sure this is a good time?" she countered.

"It's the perfect time. Rusty's out of town and I'm stuck on house arrest."

"It's going to end up being a pretty small affair." She sounded as low as Asher felt.

They hadn't spoken much since he'd been released from jail, but he'd texted her often to check in. Despite still smarting over the way she'd turned her back on him, they were family and he loved her.

"Even if there's only twenty or thirty people, it will be a party." Easing up on the forced optimism, he added, "And I really need this."

"I'll see what I can do."

She grudgingly offered suggestions for a fun-filled, family-friendly barbecue with a guest list including their usual complement of friends from the Texas Cattleman's Club—or at least the ones who were still talking to them—but also those in Royal who'd suffered because of what happened with the festival. Fearing that no one would show up if they thought he was involved, he suggested that she leave his name off the invitation.

Fifteen minutes after he'd hung up with Gina, Ross's number lit up Asher's phone.

"A *party*?" Ross demanded. "Are you out of your mind? This is no time to celebrate anything."

It wasn't a celebration, but a distraction. A way to keep from brooding over the implosion of his relationship with Lani and the bleak future that lay ahead of him.

"I'm stuck here alone with nothing to do," Asher complained.

"You're on house arrest," Ross snapped. "I don't think throwing parties is going to enhance your reputation."

"I'm not throwing a party. You and Gina are."

Asher hadn't really expected his brother to understand. Practical Ross had never related to the restlessness that drove Asher. His identity had always been cemented in being the heir to one of the wealthiest men in the country. That Ross suffered the same neglect as Asher didn't negate the blood bond.

"This isn't a good idea."

"No, it's a *great* idea." And one that Asher hoped would prove to Lani that he would make an excellent partner for her. "Oh, and make sure you invite Billy. It wouldn't be a party without him."

Eleven

Still reeling from the fight with Asher the day before, Lani buckled herself into her seat for the three-hour flight from Dallas to Las Vegas. Her stomach flipped as her phone rang. Hoping it was Asher, she glanced down at the screen but the caller was Kingston Blue.

"Hey," she began as the plane filled up around her. "I'm on my way to Vegas,"

She'd snagged a window seat and watched the grounds crew load luggage under the plane. Since she only needed a few necessities for her quick trip, her own bag sat in the compartment above her head.

"What's in Las Vegas?" Kingston Blue asked, his voice hard and suspicious.

Apparently her people skills were in the toilet. Not only had she damaged her relationship with Asher, but her credibility with her client was dangling by a thread.

"A woman by the name of Antoinette Holmes," Lani explained. "She's Billy Holmes's mother."

A charged silence radiated from the phone. She gnawed on her lip, imagining the grim tension in Kingston's face. As much as she didn't want to argue with the musician, she believed in her investigative skills *and* in Asher's innocence.

"Look, I know you don't agree with the direction I'm taking the investigation, but you hired me to find the money and I really don't think Asher's your guy." Her voice heated as her confidence flared. "If you want me off the case, I understand, but I'm still going to investigate Billy Holmes."

"How much of this has to do with your personal relationship with Asher Edmond?" While the edge had come off Kingston's tone, he sounded no less dubious. "You were in love with him once. Can you assure me that's not interfering with your judgment now?"

Lani breathed a sigh of relief that her client was willing to hear her out. This she could handle. After all, for the last five years she'd been telling herself that falling for Asher had been a huge mistake and one thing she never did was screw up twice.

"When you first approached me with the job, I wanted him to be guilty. Things didn't end well between us and I thought maybe he was finally going to have to take responsibility for a mistake he'd made."

Initially, she'd intended to demonstrate to her treacherous heart that Asher was a lying, manipulative, selfish jerk who'd toyed with her for fun and thus banish him from her daydreams forever.

"So what changed?" Kingston asked.

"I'm a professional. I approached this case by looking at the facts." Never mind that one glimpse of Asher looking exhausted and defeated in that jail cell had started to change the polarity of her emotions. "Which resulted in me interviewing several people and finding out that Billy Holmes had a sketchy past and an odd fixation on Rusty Edmond."

"But what does any of that mean?"

"I don't know, but I'm hoping to find some answers by talking to his mother."

"Fine. Keep me updated."

Lani ended the call, relieved that the musician appeared appeased for the moment. As the announcement came to stow all electronic devices, her mind went back to the last conversation she'd had with Asher. She recognized that letting him think his father had hired her had been a mistake. When she landed in Las Vegas, she would let him know that she'd spoken with Kingston and relayed her opinion about Asher no longer being her prime suspect.

Not that she believed this would be enough for him to forgive her. She hadn't understood about the strained relationship between Rusty and his adopted son or the pain Asher had felt at being either ignored or criticized by the only father figure he'd ever had.

As the plane taxied toward the runway, she closed her eyes and mentally reviewed what she'd dug up on Billy Holmes.

He'd grown up in Las Vegas, raised by a single mom.

Without any luggage to pick up at baggage claim, Lani secured a rental car and was on her way to meet Billy's mom. Antoinette Holmes was a cocktail waitress at a downtown casino and lived just east of the city center in a second-floor apartment in an older complex.

Lani was careful not to trip on the chipped concrete as she strode past a pool in desperate need of refurbishing. Feeling the heat radiating off the sun-bleached door of apartment number twelve, Lani used the corner of her phone, instead of her knuckles, to rap.

The face of the woman who answered the door looked much older than fifty-nine beneath her heavy makeup. Years of harsh desert sunshine and hard living had taken its toll on Antoinette's skin. Yet Lani could tell Billy's mother had once been a beauty.

"Antoinette Holmes?" Lani spoke the woman's name like a question although she already knew the answer.

"Yes?" The woman rested her left hand on her hip. Her slender fingers were tipped with long bright blue nails adorned with rhinestones. They matched her blue workout pants and matching sports bra. Antoinette's face might've showed her age, but her trim body did not.

"My name is Lani Li. I'm a private investigator from Dallas, Texas, and I was wondering if I could speak to you for a few minutes."

When she had indicated she was from Texas, Antoinette's eyebrows had risen. Now, however, as she raked her gaze over Lani's jeans, pale blue T-shirt and boots, the older woman's expression shifted from surprise to caution.

"What about?"

Not wanting to fidget and give Antoinette any sense that this inquiry was anything other than routine, Lani resisted the urge to wipe at the sweat trickling down her temple. Dallas had been in the upper eighties when she'd left. Las Vegas was already well into triple-digit temperatures and the heat index continued to climb as the sun crept toward its zenith in a cloudless sky of vivid blue.

"I'm doing some background work on your son, Billy," Lani declared blandly. "And I have a few questions only you can answer."

"What sort of questions?" The waitress looked poised to slam the door in Lani's face if she didn't like the answer.

Lani suspected she'd get nowhere if she told the truth. "Did you know your son has been living in Royal, Texas, for the past two years? He's staying in a guesthouse at Elegance Ranch, a property owned by Russell Edmond."

The thing about wearing long false eyelashes was that they called attention to a woman's eyes and what Lani glimpsed in Antoinette's wide green gaze was longing, anger and a trace of fear.

"I haven't seen or heard from that boy in years so I don't know what I can tell you." The older woman studied Lani for a few seconds longer while curiosity and reluctance battled on her face. In the end Antoinette backed into the house with a curt gesture that invited without being welcoming. "You might as well come in. I don't need to be air-conditioning the neighborhood."

"Thanks."

Crossing into the dim interior of the woman's apartment was like stepping back in time. And not in a good way. Years of cigarette smoke clung to the '70s wallpaper and burgundy carpet beneath her feet. As Lani made her way across the grungy patchwork of spills and threadbare spots, she couldn't help but contrast the shabby one-bedroom apartment to the elegant guesthouse on Elegance Ranch where Billy lived.

"Can I get you something to drink?" Antoinette asked, leaving Lani to wonder if she was being hospitable or if a lifetime of waitressing made the offer a habit. "I've got diet soda or water, or I could make some coffee."

"I'll take a soda," she said with a polite smile after glancing at the dishes piled in the sink. Hopefully the drink would come in a can because she couldn't imagine there was a single clean glass in the place.

After Lani perched on the gold velvet couch her hostess had indicated, Antoinette headed into the kitchen to fetch the offered drink. This gave Lani a chance to glance around. Billy's mom said she hadn't heard from him in years. Obviously she hadn't benefited from any of the money he'd swindled as Bond Howard, Bobby Hammond or Brad Howell.

Spying a cluster of pictures on a side table, Lani leaned over to peer at them. What she saw caused her to pull out her phone and snap several images.

These were obviously a collection of Antoinette's most cherished photos. They told her story, starting with a grainy shot of a somber-faced man and his beaming bride on their wedding day. Her parents, based on the fashion and quality of the photo.

Next in order was a shot of a fresh-faced teenage Antoinette, posing in a cheer uniform with two other girls similarly dressed. The trio triumphantly held a trophy in their grasp, indicating Antoinette had known better times.

Lani's favorite of the bunch was a charming image of the woman snuggling a boy of about four or five. From his mother's joyful smile, Billy hadn't lacked affection growing up. But the photo that stopped Lani's breath was the one in a fancy gold frame. It featured a beaming Antoinette and a much-younger Rusty Edmond.

"That's my boy," Antoinette said, handing Lani an off-brand diet soda before indicating a wall of photos from Billy's school years. "The last picture I took of him was the day he went off to college." She gave a bitter laugh that turned into a classic smoker's cough. "First one in my family to go."

"You must be very proud of him…" Lani trailed off, hoping Billy's mom would fill in the details without the need for direct questions.

"It gave him airs." Antoinette stared at the pictures on the side table. "What sort of background check are you doing on my boy?"

Lani resisted the urge to clear her throat. "The man who hired me is very particular about the people he does business with." It wasn't a lie. Kingston Blue had certainly had her checked out before hiring her.

"I haven't seen Billy in five years or so. He never came back much after he graduated college. Just walked away, as all men do…as his father did." Antoinette darted a glance at the man framed in gold. "I should've known better."

"Does Billy have much to do with his dad?"

Speculation gleamed in Antoinette's narrowed eyes. "Why do you need to know something like that?"

"It fills out the picture…"

The older woman assessed Lani's appearance once more. "I've said all I'm going to for free."

She blinked. "I'm sorry?"

"If you're a private detective, you've probably got an expense account." The waitress licked her lips and smiled. "If you want to know anything more, it's gonna cost you."

With Asher's freedom on the line, Lani had a lot riding on this interview, and a photo of Rusty Edmond with Billy's mother demonstrated there was a story here. To persuade the authorities to look at Billy, she needed something that piqued their interest.

Moving with deliberate intent, Lani opened her purse and added up everything she had. Would nine crisp one-hundred-dollar bills be enough to get all the information she needed? Lani pulled out one bill and set it on the coffee table in between them.

"Does Billy see his dad?"

Antoinette's hand shot out and drew the hundred toward her. The bill disappeared into her ample cleavage.

"No."

Trying not to let her impatience get the better of her, Lani plucked out another bill and set it on the table. She made sure to avoid glancing at the cluster of pictures as she asked, "Does his father know about Billy?"

"He knew I was pregnant, but he didn't believe Billy was his."

So the answer to that was no. The photo of his mother with Russell Edmond was the only one of Antoinette with a man. Billy obviously knew or suspected that Rusty was his father. What was Billy up to? Why hadn't he told Rusty that they were father and son?

"Why not?"

Antoinette crossed her arms over her chest and scowled. Another bill appeared in Lani's hand. She set it on the table.

"Tell me about Billy's father." She gestured at the picture in the gold frame. "Is this him?"

"A real charmer with a sexy drawl. He was from Texas like you. An oilman with deep pockets. Good tipper." The waitress purred, "He made me feel like the most beautiful woman on the planet."

While the woman relived what was obviously a high point in her life, Lani couldn't help but notice the similarity to how she'd met Asher. Antoinette waxed nostalgic about Rusty's hypnotic gray eyes and how his deep laugh had given her chills. Meanwhile Lani pictured how Asher had hungrily watched her through half-closed lids and wore down her resistance with his lingering, sensual smiles. "He liked to come to the casino where I worked and throw money around. He treated me good."

"That's great," she murmured, growing uncomfortable at their parallel experiences.

Yet was it a surprise that when a wealthy man wanted a woman, he used whatever means at his disposal to have her?

"Until I got pregnant," Antoinette said. "Then it was over."

Abruptly Lani felt sorry for the woman. If she and Asher hadn't been careful, that might've been her, pregnant and scared with an uncertain future looming before her. Given his restless nature and frat-boy attitude, would Asher have reacted any better to an unplanned pregnancy than his father had?

At least she knew things would be different today. If she got pregnant, she had no doubt that Asher would not only want to be an involved father, he'd probably insist on taking care of her, as well.

The thought warmed her. Even though she let him believe her opinion of him hadn't changed, the concern he'd shown for those harmed by the troubles surrounding the festival demonstrated that he could care about someone besides himself. And really, if she took a good honest look at everything that had transpired between them that summer on Appaloosa Island, she knew she never would've fallen for him if he hadn't treated her so well. In fact, once she stopped getting in her own way, she'd discovered that Asher made her feel secure.

Lani plucked the rest of her cash out of her wallet and placed it on the table. "This is everything I have. Just answer these last few questions." And then without waiting for Antoinette to agree, she launched into the rest of her inquiry. "Did you ask him for child support?"

"Never thought of it."

That was so obviously a lie, but Lani resisted the urge to challenge Antoinette.

"But you said he was wealthy. I would think you could've proved Billy was his son and benefited financially. How come you didn't run a paternity test?"

Suddenly Antoinette didn't look so eager to keep going. "You ask a lot of questions."

"I paid you a lot of money for answers," Lani countered in aggrieved tones as frustration got the better of her. Asher was counting on her to save him and everything hinged on what she found out. "Why no paternity test?" she repeated, slapping her hand over the pile of cash as the waitress leaned forward to snatch it up.

Antoinette kept her gaze riveted on the money as she mumbled, "There were other men around the same time."

Yet a paternity test would've provided definitive proof of whether or not Rusty was Billy's dad. Unless…

"How much did he pay you to leave him alone and forget about the paternity test?"

"You think you're so smart, don't you?" Antoinette snarled. She glanced at the money again and heaved a sigh. "Fine. He paid me ten grand to drop it and never contact him again. And Russell wasn't the sort of man you crossed."

"So, you don't actually know who Billy's father is," Lani mused.

But Antoinette obviously hoped it was Russell Edmond. The ornate gold frame around the oil magnate's image highlighted how much he'd meant to her. Billy had grown up seeing that face every day. It made perfect sense that he'd believe this man was his father.

Had resentment festered with each passing year? Growing up poor, had Billy become obsessed about his wealthy father living in Texas? Had he planned how he was going to make friends with his half brother and eventually worm his way into the family?

"Does Billy begrudge his father for not acknowledging him?"

"No. Why would he?" But something about Antoinette's answer didn't ring true for Lani.

With one last glance at the photo of Rusty and Antoinette, Lani lifted her hand off the cash and got to her feet. After a quick goodbye and no backward glance, Lani escaped the suffocating apartment with her thoughts whirling from all she'd learned. Finally Billy's motive was clear. Not only had he taken revenge on his father's family, but he'd also pulled off the biggest score of his life.

No doubt he wouldn't be sticking around for much longer. In fact Lani was surprised he'd stayed in town this long. With that thought came a rush of panic. She needed to get back to Royal as soon as possible and convince the authorities to take what she'd discovered and go after Billy. But first she needed to reach out to the one person who would benefit the most from what she'd learned.

This might be enough to save Asher and she couldn't wait to tell him.

But two hours and three phone calls later, Asher hadn't picked up once.

As her plane for Dallas began boarding, Lani ended the last call without leaving a third message. She was determined not to jump to the wrong conclusions as to why he wasn't answering her calls. But even so, anxiety sank its talons into her psyche, making her wince. There were a lot of possibilities for why he wasn't picking up beyond the one currently stuck in the forefront of her mind—that she'd hurt him badly. Badly enough that he wanted nothing more to do with her? Lani desperately hoped not.

Asher couldn't take his gaze off Ross, Charlotte and Ben. He'd never envied his brother as much as he did at this moment. That could've been him with Lani and possibly their own child if he hadn't been so afraid of the changes required to move forward with their relationship. Without offering her any sort of vision of an alternative, better future with him, he'd selfishly asked her to change her plans for grad school and follow him to Argentina and beyond. Was it any wonder that she'd balked? He'd known how driven she was.

If he'd put some thought into a plan, he might have found a better way to convince her than, *I have plenty of money. You'll never need to work a day in your life.*

He'd known immediately that was the wrong tact to take with her. But it wasn't like he could set his heart at her feet, tell her he'd fallen hard and couldn't bear to live without her. What if it didn't last? What if she woke up and realized he wasn't good enough for her? He'd dreaded the possibility that the love shining in her eyes would dim as disappointment set in.

She'd stopped criticizing his lifestyle once they'd started dating, but her desire to help people and her passion for justice was all he needed to recognize that she didn't approve of his lack of direction any more than Rusty did. And at the end of summer, when she left Appaloosa Island to live her mission-driven life, he'd been left wondering why he always seemed to be craving the love and approval of people who could never accept him for who he was.

Lately he'd been wondering a great deal about what might've happened back then if he had changed. Grown up. Become the man Lani needed. Would she have started to take him seriously? Would they have gotten married? Had a child? He'd sure wanted to be with her.

To demonstrate what life with him could be like, he'd taken her on a magical journey through the extravagances his lifestyle afforded him. The big boat, fine dining and luxurious suites at the best hotels, a private plane to anywhere they wanted to go… But he'd mistaken her delight in the finer things he offered with a shift in her nature. She might've been able to appreciate the amenities he had access to, but that didn't mean those things would become more important to her than her schooling and the career in law enforcement she'd hoped to pursue.

"It's good to see Ross this happy, isn't it?"

While he's been observing the happy family, Gina had walked up beside him. Despite her upbeat statement, she looked as gloomy as Asher felt. He threw his arm around her in comfort. Over the course of Lani's investigation into the missing festival money, Asher and his sister had made a semblance of peace.

"Obviously fatherhood and being in love suit him." Asher noted a roughness to his voice. He swallowed a hard knot in his throat before musing, "Do you suppose either one of us has that to look forward to?"

"I don't know about you," Gina murmured, "but I'm pretty sure I don't."

"Why is that?" Asher turned his full attention on his sister and seeing her misery, took her hand in his. Squeezing gently in reassurance, he said, "You never know. Mr. Right could be waiting for you to notice him."

She responded with a bitter laugh. "With our family's reputation sullied by the festival scandal, who could possibly want me now?"

"Any man with half a brain would realize what a catch you are," Asher said, surprised by his sister's inability to see her worth. "There's more to you than being an Edmond. You know that, right?"

Not only was Gina beautiful and smart, she was kind and giving, as well. That she failed to recognize all she had to offer wasn't a surprise. None of the three siblings had been showered with the sort of approval and love that would've given them the confidence to take on the world. Rusty never acted as if he gave a damn about any of them. Was it any wonder the three of them struggled to find love and develop successful relationships?

"I really don't," Gina said. "I guess I never realized how much I benefited from being an Edmond until our name got dragged through the mud."

"I'm sorry this happened."

His sister looked stricken. "I know you. Stealing isn't your style. I feel bad that I ever believed you were guilty."

"Don't worry about it," Asher assured her with a warm smile. "The evidence was so damning that there were times I actually thought I had stolen the funds."

"Oh, Asher." She laughed at his joke as he'd hoped she would and his spirits remained high even as she sobered once more. "But what are we going to do about proving your innocence?"

"Lani and I have some ideas on that. In fact, we have a suspect."

Gina looked startled. "Who?"

He'd promised Lani not to tell Ross what they learned about Billy, but he could share the information with Gina without violating their agreement.

"We've been looking into Billy."

"Billy Holmes?" Her voice was louder and sharper than Asher would've liked and he immediately shushed her. "Why him?"

"We found out he's been operating under false names all over the country and getting women to invest in schemes before backing out and taking their money with him."

"Seriously?" she gasped, confusion blanketing her expression. "That makes no sense! He's been Ross's friend since college. I can't imagine him doing something like that or being that type of person without Ross realizing it."

Asher pondered how Rusty had embraced Billy when the cranky billionaire rarely approved of anyone, including his own children. "Well, he's obviously pretty good at charming people to get what he wants. I mean, he *is* currently living in the guesthouse on our estate."

"What does Ross have to say about this?"

"I haven't spoken to him about it and I need for you to promise me that you won't say anything either. I can't risk him tipping off Billy. He's already left a trail of missing funds across the country. Nothing on the scale of what was stolen from Soiree on the Bay, but it has all led up to this moment. And with me in jail, he gets away with it."

Gina's brown eyes grew wider as he spoke and Asher realized his voice had grown louder as he vented his frustration.

"You need to go to the authorities with this," his sister said, her eyes darting toward Ross and his family.

"With what?" Asher growled. "It's nothing but

speculation at this point. I have no proof." Then he remembered that Lani had called him before the party started. Still smarting from their last conversation, he'd never picked up her calls or listened to her messages. He pulled out his phone and unlocked the screen. "Or maybe we do. Lani called me from Vegas."

"What was she doing there?"

"That's where Billy's mom lives. She went to see what she could find out. I haven't listened to her message."

"You've been with her a lot. I heard she moved in for a while," Gina remarked, her voice carefully neutral. "Is it all business? I mean, when you two dated before, it was pretty clear she meant a lot to you."

"It's not business on my part," he retorted, his clipped tone exposing his raw emotions. "She just doesn't see a future for us."

"Because...? I mean you were once in love, right?"

"Yes. And my feelings haven't changed on that front." Even though he was confessing to the wrong woman, it felt good to admit how he felt about Lani. "I just don't think I'm the man she wants."

"So become that man." Gina's advice was simple and hard-hitting. "That girl looked at you with heart emoji in her eyes. I'm sure if you put in the effort, she'd come around."

With his lungs constricting in reaction to his sister's words, Asher drew Gina into a hug and then hit the Play button on his phone.

Lani's voice came over the speaker, sounding excited and somewhat annoyed. "Will you please stop avoiding my calls? I know you're not unavailable so I guess I'm just gonna have to leave another message. I talked to Billy's mom and it turns out she had an affair with Rusty. He gave her ten thousand and told her to never contact him again. The thing is, she has no proof that Billy is Rusty's son. She never had a chance to do a paternity test and apparently there were several men she was seeing around the same time. I guess that explains Billy why was so unhappy when Ross and Rusty looked like they were getting along and why he set you up. He thinks he's Rusty son and resents the fact that he didn't have all the things growing up that you all did… Well, the plane's getting ready to take off so they're making me shut off my phone. I'll arrive in Dallas in three hours. I'll call you when I land and we can talk more then."

The whole time Lani had been speaking, he'd been staring at the screen. Now he looked up at his sister and saw his shock mirrored on her face.

"Wow," Gina said in awe.

"Wow is right."

"Now we have to talk to Ross. And tell the authorities."

"Absolutely." But his attention was on the dark-haired man making for the exit in a hurry. "Except I think we might be out of time." He indicated Billy's rapid departure.

Gina's eyes rounded. "Do you think he heard us?"

"Maybe." To Asher's relief, Billy's progress was halted by a trio of women. "Can you keep him busy for me? I need fifteen minutes."

"Where are you going?"

Asher thought about his apartment over the barn and the unlocked front door giving access to anyone on the property. "I'm going to search the guesthouse."

Twelve

The distance between the main house and the guest-house where Billy currently resided was a three-minute jog along a tree-lined winding drive. Asher accomplished it in half the time. Heart pounding, his breath coming hard from the sprint, he trotted up the steps to the front door, keyed in the code to unlock the door and entered.

The house's cool stillness embraced him. Asher knew the housekeeper wasn't home. Anytime there was a party at the main house, she joined the staff, keeping the food and drinks flowing smoothly from the kitchen to the guests.

Still, running into someone was the least of his problems. He had no clear idea where to begin a search and a limited amount of time to execute it. What did he hope to find? A laptop with incriminating information would be great but he'd settle for a file marked *stolen festival funds*.

When they'd landed on Billy as a prime suspect, he'd proposed to Lani that they infiltrate the guest-house while Billy was away, but she'd shut him down. Her methodical approach didn't involve breaking and entering. But it wasn't really breaking in when he had the code to the front door, right?

Asher made his way into the study off the foyer. He couldn't believe his luck. A laptop sat on the large wood desk and he made his way over to it. Even as he lifted the top and peered at the screen, he had to wonder if this was just a decoy. Surely Billy was too clever to leave a bunch of damning evidence lying around for someone to scoop up and run out the door with.

Seconds rushed by as Asher pulled up the browser history and quickly scanned through it. Asher couldn't see where Billy had used this computer to access any banks. Still, his search had been cursory at best and with time running out he looked around for a place to stash the laptop. If Billy intended to pack up and get out of town, Asher wanted to make sure he wouldn't be able to take this device with him. The quickest, most obvious spot was underneath the couch cushions. He was counting on the man assuming someone had walked off with the computer and that he wouldn't search the room.

The bedrooms were on a level above and Asher headed up the stairs, taking them two at a time. He found an identical laptop to the one downstairs, sand-wiched between the box spring and mattress. With ex-citement pumping adrenaline through his bloodstream, he slid the computer into a laptop case that he found in the closet. With the thrill of the hunt surging, he riffled through the nightstand and dresser before getting even more creative with the search. From their careful concealment beneath shirts and socks, taped to the back of the drawer and even affixed behind the painting over the bed, he unearthed several passports—one with Billy's face but Asher's name that he dropped into his pocket—along with a wad of cash, two burner phones and a handgun.

This was *not* how an innocent man behaved.

Asher glanced at the closet, wondering how many goodies he could turn up there, but heard the front door open. With only one set of stairs leading up to the second floor, he was trapped. Fortunately he'd left everything except for the laptop where he'd found it. Asher eased out of the master suite and crossed the landing to one of the two guest bedrooms just as he heard Billy start to climb upstairs. With his blood thundering in his ears, he slipped behind the door out of sight and wondered if he dared try to slip down the stairs while Billy was packing.

Instead Asher glanced at the window. Maybe he could try to jump and hope he landed without hurting himself. Moving cautiously, he went to the window and opened it. He hadn't done more than drop the laptop into the bushes below before Billy started cursing. Asher barely had time to press himself against the wall when the other man raced past again.

Deciding this was his best chance to make his escape, and with his ears tuned for the slightest noise, Asher waited until he heard the front door open and close once more. Then he quickly, but quietly, descended to the first floor. After a quick detour to the study to collect the laptop, he headed for the kitchen and the door that led to the side yard. He needed to retrieve the other laptop, but when he opened the door, standing before him was Billy Holmes with a handgun leveled at his chest.

"You."

Asher was not at all flattered at the surprise on Billy's face. "Me."

Billy's gaze went to the laptop Asher held. "Give that to me."

"Or what? You'll shoot me?" He was rethinking his words as the other man smirked. "Fire that gun and everyone at the house will hear. Gina knows what you did. She's probably already warned Ross. They'll lock the gates and you'll never get out."

"I guess I need a little insurance then, don't I?" Billy backed up and gestured with the gun toward the car parked in the driveway.

Unsure what the traitor had in mind, Asher decided to let the scene play out until he saw an opening to act. A suitcase stood beside the car. Keeping a close eye on Asher, Billy popped open the trunk.

"Give me the laptop and get in."

"The trunk?"

Asher took a tighter grip on the laptop, prepared to swing it at Billy's head, but the other man shook his head.

"Don't be stupid. If you make me shoot you, I might not get away, but you'll definitely be dead."

All too aware that would be true, Asher made a huge

show of reluctance before handing over what he hoped was Billy's decoy computer.

"Get in," Billy repeated.

"Why? You have everything you need to get away clean."

"Except for a head start. So, to throw everyone into a state of confusion, you and I are going for a little drive."

And before Asher could summon another protest, Billy's hand holding the gun shot out and everything went black.

No three-hour plane ride had ever felt as long as this one.

How could she have told Asher he wasn't the right man for her? *Of course* he was. She loved him just the way he was. She didn't want to change him. Why would she? He was thrilling and adventurous and made her get out of her head and listen to her heart. Loving him was a wonderful chaotic ride and she was ready to spend the rest of her life on it.

The first thing she would do when she saw him again was tell him that she loved him. No matter if he was angry with her or indifferent. She wouldn't hesitate, wouldn't play it safe. If he believed that the only reason she'd been waiting to speak up was to determine if he was innocent, she'd convince him that her change of heart had come the day they'd visited the festival site on Appaloosa Island. She'd just been too afraid to trust her emotions.

As soon as the plane landed, Lani turned her phone back on and watched the screen light up with notifications. She scanned for a message from Asher, but the only names that appeared were Ross, Gina and the Maverick County Sheriff's Department.

Cursing the love of her life for being impossibly stubborn, Lani dialed his number again and groaned in frustration when it rolled straight into voice mail. With Asher out of reach, she turned her attention to the rest of her messages, starting with Gina.

We think Billy overheard your voice mail. Ross and Asher are going to talk to him.

"Damn it!"

Lani's seatmate shot her a dark look and she offered the woman a tight smile and a mumbled apology as she checked the time stamp and saw that it had come in an hour earlier.

And as if that wasn't bad enough, she had three messages from Ross, each one worse than the last.

Billy knows we're onto him and he's running.

Asher went to the guesthouse to stop him.

I'm not sure what's going on, but Sheriff Battle just called to say that Asher is on the run.

What the hell was going on? Lani dialed Ross's number, but after several rings it rolled to voice mail the way Asher's had. She scrolled through her contacts and located the one for the Maverick County Sheriff's Department. Tapping her fingers against the armrest, she waited for someone to pick up.

"I'm looking for Sheriff Battle," Lani said when the receptionist answered. "My name is Lani Li and it's about Asher Edmond."

"One moment."

With hold music playing in her ear, Lani stared out the window as the plane taxied toward the busy Dallas/Fort Worth terminal, stopping repeatedly to let other planes pass. Her heart thudded hard against her ribs as her agitation grew by the second.

What had Asher been thinking to go after Billy? Didn't he know he was already in enough trouble? He and Ross should've called the sheriff and let the cops sort everything out. But sitting idly by when there was something adventurous to do wasn't Asher's style.

"Sheriff Battle." The man's calm, booming voice did little to soothe Lani's wildly fluctuating emotions.

"Sheriff, this is Lani Li. I've just landed in Dallas and I think I know who embezzled the money from the Soiree on the Bay festival and set up Asher Edmond to take the fall."

"I don't think you've heard, Ms. Li, but Asher Edmond is running."

"He's not running because he's not guilty." Lani couldn't imagine what had possessed Asher to take this sort of risk. What was he doing? This might ruin everything. "I think what he may be doing is trying to stop Billy Holmes from leaving town and disappearing."

"What does Mr. Holmes have to do with any of this?"

"I went to Las Vegas to visit Billy's mother. I found a connection there to Rusty Edmond."

A moment of silence followed her words, and then Sheriff Battle said, "Maybe you'd better fill me in…"

By the time she finished explaining everything, the plane had reached the terminal and the woman in the seat next to her was openly goggling. Lani ignored the eavesdropper and willed the passengers to disembark at a faster pace.

"So, you can see why Billy Holmes has to be stopped and questioned," she added, completely out of breath. "It's why Asher is chasing after him."

"If that's true, then they're both heading to the airport," the sheriff said.

"Billy can't get away." If that happened, the money would be gone forever and Asher's name might never be cleared.

"I'll get ahold of the special agents in charge of the case and my deputy that's following Asher and fill them in."

Lani hung up the call and got to her feet. As she joined the line of disembarking passengers, she chided herself for not calling the investigators before boarding the plane in Las Vegas. Yet how was she supposed to know that Asher would do something as reckless as go after Billy on his own? She ground her teeth as the people in front of her slowly shuffled off the plane. When she got ahold of Asher, she was going to kill him. Or kiss him senseless.

Once she reached the terminal, Lani looped her bag over her shoulder and began to jog toward the security gate that led to the arrivals area. She had no luggage, and no reason to follow the crowd to baggage claim. Besides, if Billy and Asher were on their way to the airport, the most likely spot to find them would be at the ticketing level. Only as she passed the doors leading to the shuttle that circled the five different terminals did the magnitude of the search area sap her hope. How could she hope to find Billy amongst the dozens of airlines and thousands of people checking in?

She was racing toward the arrivals area, scanning the faces around her, when she spied a familiar figure exiting TSA. Although he was wearing sunglasses and a baseball cap, she recognized Billy Holmes.

She angled in his direction, moving fast to intercept him. It wasn't until she stepped into his path that Lani realized she hadn't considered how to stop him.

"Billy Holmes."

To Lani's relief, he stopped.

His icy blue gaze darted in all directions before coming to rest on her. "Do I know you?"

"I'm Lani Li. I've been hired by Kingston Blue to look into the missing funds from the Soiree on the Bay festival."

His upper lip lifted in a snarl. "Good for you."

"I'd like to talk to you about your connection with the Edmond family."

"I'm sorry, but I have a plane to catch and don't have time to—"

Billy side stepped as if to go around her, but Lani was prepared for his evasion and kept herself in his path.

"I visited your mother today," she told him, hoping if she delayed Billy long enough, the police might catch up to him. "I know her connection to Rusty Edmond."

Billy shrugged. "They had an affair. So what?"

"So, you think he's your father. You think he abandoned you and your mother and you wanted payback.

That's why you stole the money from the festival and blamed Asher."

"That's ridiculous. Asher stole that money. Everyone knows that." He gave her a cocky smile, but tension rode every line of his body.

"I also know about Bond Howard, Bobby Hammond and Brad Howell."

"Who?" Billy continued to regard her as if she were out of her mind, but Lani saw she had his complete attention.

Her cell phone began to ring. Hoping it was Asher, she glanced down at the screen, but realized it was Ross Edmond. She answered the call, but by the time she glanced back up at Billy, he was gone.

"Damn it!" she growled.

"Lani? Is that you?" Ross sounded upset and confused.

"Yes. Where's Asher?" she demanded, searching all around her for Billy. She couldn't spot his tall figure anywhere. It was as if the man had vanished.

"He's being arrested."

Anxiety banished all thought of Billy Holmes from her mind. She had to get to Asher. "Where are you?"

"Outside Terminal A."

As luck would have it, Lani's plane from Las Vegas had landed at the same terminal.

She ran outside and gaped at the mob scene. Four police cars surrounded a sedan parked by the curb with its trunk open. They had one man down on the ground as another argued and waved his arm toward the terminal. It took her a second to realize that Ross Edmond was the one gesticulating wildly and Asher was face down on the pavement, his hands cuffed behind his back.

She ran over and added her voice to the cacophony. "Billy Holmes is in the terminal. I just saw him. He's getting away."

Ross turned to her with a relieved expression. "That's what I'm trying to tell them," he said, "but they're not listening to me."

Two cops lifted Asher to his feet. One wore the insignia of the Maverick County Sheriff's Department, the other was a state trooper.

"I was kidnapped," Asher protested, eyes widening as he spotted her. "Hey, Lani."

As she rushed toward him, the state trooper stepped in her way and stood with his feet planted shoulder-width apart, hands on his gun belt. "And you are?"

"Lani Li. I called and spoke with Sheriff Battle when I landed." She glanced at the deputy's name tag. "Deputy Vesta, didn't the sheriff get ahold of you? You have the wrong man."

"I don't think so," the deputy said, jerking his thumb at Asher. "He's trying to get away." His vehement glare suggested that there was something personal in his dislike of Asher.

"Look, I wasn't trying to escape." He tipped his head to one side, showing a bloody gash on his temple. "The bastard bashed me on the head and dumped me in the trunk."

"You weren't in the trunk when we pulled up." The state trooper pointed out.

"Because the car had finally stopped and I figured it was safe for me to get out."

"The man you're looking for is Billy Holmes," Lani put in, tearing her gaze from Asher's wound. She hoped it wasn't as serious as it looked.

"Don't know anything about that," the trooper said. "We received a BOLO from Maverick County that this guy was skipping town."

Lani glanced at the car the police cruisers had surrounded. Its open trunk seemed to substantiate Asher's claim.

"He wasn't skipping town because he's innocent," Lani fumed. "You need to go after Billy Holmes. I ran into him in there. He's getting away."

The trooper glanced toward the door leading into the terminal. "Who's this Billy Holmes character?"

The deputy started dragging his prisoner toward the police car. "Let's go."

"Can't you wait just a second," Asher protested, resisting. "I have something to tell Lani."

Heartsick, she moved to go after them, but the trooper caught her arm, keeping her in place. She glanced around the police officer, trying to keep Asher in sight.

"Let me go with him."

Was that her voice sounding so desperate and anxious? Suddenly it had become crucial that Asher hear that she loved him.

"They're taking him back to Royal. You can see him at the sheriff's station."

"Please," she pleaded with the cop. "There's something he needs to know."

"Fine. Make it quick."

The Maverick County deputy was already urging

Asher into the back of his patrol car when Lani drew near. The deputy had his hand on the door and was about to slam it shut when she spoke up.

"Wait." Irrational panic had seized her and wouldn't let go. "Just give me a second with him."

To her dismay he just smirked at her and started to close the door. A fraction of a second remained for her to confess the three words that had been hiding in her heart. Terrified, where she'd been bold moments earlier, Lani locked eyes with Asher and sucked in a breath for courage. But as she began to speak, Asher clearly had something on his mind as well and there wasn't time for both.

As the car door swung on its hinges, an instant before glass and metal blocked their words, their overlapping messages reached their targets.

"I love you."

"I got Billy's laptop."

Thirteen

Asher lay on his back staring at the damn jail ceiling once again. His head was throbbing beneath the hastily applied bandage on his temple. He'd stopped pacing an hour ago and resigned himself to spending the night. At least this time he wasn't worried about being stuck here indefinitely. He'd been told that they'd found Billy's laptop where he'd hidden it and the forensics team was combing the hard drive in search of the accounts where the funds had been sent. Thanks to Lani, a clear picture had formed of Billy's notorious past, stemming from his mother's affair with Rusty that suggested a reason for him to destroy the Edmond family's reputations and set up Asher to take the fall for the missing festival funds.

Unfortunately, in the midst of the wild and completely out-of-control scene at the airport, Billy had escaped into the crowds and it appeared as if he'd vanished into thin air. No doubt he had several different identifications to go with his aliases and with the festival funds squirreled away, he had the means to go just about anywhere.

But none of that mattered anymore. What preoccupied Asher was that he was stuck in here while Lani was out there doing who knew what. He was on pins and needles waiting to be released. And after he was set free, then what? He and Lani hadn't sorted out their problems. Before leaving for Las Vegas, she'd made it clear that she still didn't trust him.

As the hours passed without any word from her, he grew almost frantic with worry. Over and over his mind replayed those moments before Deputy Vesta had shut him into the back of the patrol car. Once again Asher had screwed up. While Lani was confessing her love, he'd been bragging about securing Billy's laptop. She was sure to think that he was only worried about saving his own ass, not that he'd done it for her so that she could find the missing money and solve the case.

And now she was avoiding him, no doubt guessing that he didn't love her in return. Would she ever give him the chance to explain? Or was it already too late? Maybe she wasn't busy with the authorities. Maybe she'd already gone back to Dallas, putting him in her rearview mirror once again.

Nor could he blame her for leaving him to rot. Hell, if he'd confessed his love to her only to discover she was solely focused on saving her firm, he'd be pretty messed up too. Hopefully she would give him another chance. He would shower her with I love you's from now until eternity if she would just show up.

The door leading to the rest of the police station opened and Asher's heart gave a painful wrench. He was on his feet and across the small cell before realizing his visitor wasn't Lani, but the stocky deputy who despised him.

"Hello, Deputy Vesta," he said in his most droll tone. "I thought you'd forgotten all about me."

Vesta shot him a disgusted look. "Someone's here to see you."

Asher grabbed the bars and held on as relief washed over him. His head spun as Lani slowly advanced into the room. Strands of dark hair framed her exhausted features and her shoulders slumped as if burdened by an enormous weight. She looked as if the news she'd come to share was so bad she couldn't bear to speak it.

"What is it?" he demanded. His stomach knotted. "What's happening?"

"You look like hell," she said, stopping halfway toward him.

Her unwillingness to meet his gaze coupled with her delay in coming to see him made his heart plummet. Either she'd been unable to convince the authorities that Billy was the true thief or her part of the case was concluded and this was goodbye.

"Well I've been locked up in jail for…" without his watch or a clock to gauge the time, he'd lost track of how long he'd been in this cell "…a while now," he concluded wearily, wondering how he could possibly convince her they had a future if he remained locked up. "You, on the other hand, look glorious."

Her lips flattened into an unhappy line. "I'm tired and in desperate need of a shower so…"

More than anything he needed to touch her, to crush her in his arms and deliver his heart into her keeping. But this time he knew he needed more than his easy charm. She needed—deserved—the honest message of his heart.

"About what happened at the airport," he began.

"Billy got away." She shook her head. "We're not sure if he's actually Rusty's son, but it's clear that he believes that's the case and that he wanted Rusty—your whole family, really—to pay for abandoning him and his mother."

Asher could care less about Billy Holmes or the damned case. All he knew was that his future happiness was slipping through his fingers. He needed to be clearer, to make her understand how mad he was at himself for screwing up again. Hopefully it wasn't too late to make her understand that he regretted not speaking from his heart. It was what *she'd* done in that tense, chaotic moment. Would she believe him now?

"I don't care about that right now," he insisted, wishing she'd stop staring at his chest and see his earnest expression. He blustered on, "I want to explain about what happened when you said I love you and I told you I got Billy's laptop. What I was really trying to say was that I love you too."

After flicking her gaze to his face, she took a single step closer. Her bowed head and tightly clenched hands gave her a look of uncharacteristic uncertainty and Asher took that as his chance to spill all of it.

"I've loved you since the first time you called me

frat boy," he rushed on, baring all his fear and regret, his joy and hope. He needed his sincerity to reach her, to encourage her to give him—*them*—a chance.

He stretched out his arms as another slow, shuffling step brought her almost within reach. She continued to remain silent, but her willingness to hear him out gave him hope.

"From here on out, I'm at your command," he declared, the words tumbling out of him. She'd given him this chance and he would not fail. "Whatever you need. Whoever you need me to be. I'm that guy. I swear you will never be disappointed in me ever again."

She'd moved near enough that he could wrap his fingers around her jacket lapels and pull her forward.

"I love you," he murmured, putting his whole heart into the phrase.

Lani caught his wrists as he tugged her toward him, but to keep her balance rather than to resist him. Still, it was pretty obvious that more kept them apart than the steel metal grid between them.

"I love you just the way you are," she whispered, lifting her gaze to his at last.

The amount of anguish in her mink-brown eyes made Asher catch his breath. Throat tight, he cupped her cheek and cursed the mess he'd made of things. If only he'd been able to find the courage years ago to give her his heart.

"But I'm already different because of you," he said. "Being with you that summer five years ago changed me. Oh, I resisted. I was still an arrogant ass, asking you to give up on your dream when I wasn't ready to grow up and take responsibilities for the decisions I'd made."

He shook his head in disgust. "Looking back, I was so stupid to persist in trying to win Rusty's approval, too caught up in my resentment when I couldn't."

"We both had a lot of growing up to do." Her smile was both sad and filled with regret. "With grad school ahead of me, I wasn't ready to be in a serious relationship. I didn't think I could have it all. A successful career *and* you."

Optimistic that she hadn't barred her heart to him, the knot in his chest eased slightly. "Maybe I'm reading this wrong," he teased, "but I'm not sensing you thought being with me was gonna be a picnic."

"Oh, it would've been a picnic, all right," she muttered with a quiet snort. "Including fire ants and an unexpected thunderstorm."

"You're not wrong." He accepted the accuracy of her claim with a wry smirk. "Being with me won't be without its surprises."

When it came to consistency and predictability, he would not be her ideal choice. They approached things in completely opposite ways. She was methodical. He was spontaneous. Yet they both loved a challenge and never let fear stop them from engaging in thrilling adventures.

"At least it will never be dull." She thrust her knuckles into his stomach. The jab didn't hurt, but her message was clear. *Don't make me regret this.*

"I swear I won't," he murmured, pressing his face into the gap between the bars, but finding her lips remained out of reach. "I don't suppose there's any way you could get me out of here so we could seal our new partnership with a kiss."

"Oh," she said with a playful lilt in her voice. "Did I forget to mention that you're free to go?"

The news shot through him like a lightning bolt. "This is the second-best news I've had all day."

Her left eyebrow lifted. "And the best news?"

"Deputy Vesta promised me meat loaf for dinner."

As her eyes blazed, Asher was really glad to have the protection of the cell bars between them. A second later, however, before she could voice the murder flashing in her eyes, the aforementioned deputy reentered the room and unlocked the cell door.

"See if you can stay out of trouble this time," Vesta grumbled, looking as if he'd tasted something really bad.

With a cheeky smile for the deputy, Asher grabbed Lani's hand and pulled her toward freedom. This time, his incarceration had only been a few hours, but while waiting for Lani to come visit him, it had felt like an eternity.

He intended on making a beeline for the front door, but Lani resisted. When he looked back at her, she shook her head.

"We need to get that off first," she said, indicating the monitoring device on his ankle. "You are officially no longer a suspect in the theft of the festival funds."

Asher wrapped his arms around Lani and swept her off her feet. As he whirled her in a tight circle, she wrapped her arms around his neck and laughed merrily in his ear. Nothing had ever felt as good as her body pressed up against his, her breath warm on his neck, her joy filling him with giddy delight.

When he set Lani back on her feet and dipped his

head to hers, she rose up on tiptoe to meet him half way. Her lips parted on a groan and he sent his tongue dancing forward to meet hers. They clung together, the fierce, thrilling kiss making his head swim. His throat tightened on a rush of joy. This woman in his arms was all the contentment that had been missing from his life.

"I take back what I said earlier," he declared, breaking off the kiss. "*This* is the second-best news I've heard all day."

As he spoke, he towed her toward the room where the electronic device had been attached a month earlier. Half an hour later he emerged into the humid evening and sucked in a breath of fresh air.

"We have to celebrate my freedom," he said. "Where should we go? New York? Buenos Aires? Tahiti?"

"How about we go back to Elegance Ranch and start figuring out how this new partnership of ours is going to work."

"When you say partnership…" He held his breath, wondering what she had in mind. Did she mean a business partnership? Or a personal one?

"I've been thinking about hiring an associate and I could use someone like you with the sort of connections that could bring in a better paying clientele." Her fingers tightened on his as she added, "It doesn't pay well, but if you work really hard, we might be able to grow the business."

"I appreciate your willingness to mentor me," he teased, drawing her toward the parking lot, eager to get her alone and show her without words just how much he adored her. "And I am grateful for your faith in me, but…"

"But?" she prompted, doubt creeping into her tone.

"But…" They reached her SUV and she reached into her pocket for the keys. "I have a little different take on our partnership," Drawing her into his arms, he lowered his forehead to hers. "One that involves rings and vows and kids. To summarize, it's us living happily-ever-after."

Lani chewed on her lower lip for several suspenseful seconds before her lashes lifted and she met his gaze. "Are you sure you're ready to take on that sort of partnership?"

"I've been thinking about it a lot. Someone needs to keep me in line. And I think you'll agree that no one is better at it than you." He grew serious as he stared into her eyes, willing her to see the fervent truth of his love. "And then there's the part where I adore you and can't bear to live without you. I want us to have kids and be a happy family."

The words came faster and faster as her muscles tensed. She seemed reluctant to take him seriously and his breath grew ragged as a tight band around his chest kept his lungs from fully expanding.

"I know this may seem like it's coming too soon. What can I say to convince you I can't live without you?" A lightbulb went off in his head and he dropped to one knee before her. Taking her hand in his, he offered her solemn sincerity. "Lani Li, I offer you my heart. Will you accept?"

To his dismay, she began to laugh.

"What's so funny? I'm trying to be all romantic."

"This is you being romantic?" She twisted her features into a skeptical expression, but a slight twitch at the corner of her mouth hinted at a smile.

"Give me a chance," he rasped. "Marry me."

For several heartbeats the only sound between them was the harsh, irregular pattern of their breathing. As he waited out the silence, Asher knew this wasn't the moment that would make or break them. He wasn't going to give up if she said no. She was too important to him to so readily accept defeat. He would fight for her. Fight for the amazing future they would have. But when her words came, it became clear that any battle she intended to wage would be at his side.

"Yes. I'll marry you."

Relief slammed into him. Leaping to his feet, he banded one arm around her waist and startled her with a quick spin and a dip. "At last you'll be mine."

"I've always been yours," she gasped. "Now, can I please get up?"

He set her back on her feet, but kept her in his arms. Setting aside all levity, he cupped the side of her face. "I'm done with running away because I'm too scared to face rejection. I intend to stay put and put in the effort."

"I love you, Asher Davidson Edmond." She framed his face with her palms and set fire to his blood with her earnest gaze. "I'm sorry I didn't give us a chance five years ago. I was afraid to choose you over my career because I didn't trust what we had could be enough. I never even considered fighting to have both. I know now that my life isn't fulfilling without you in it. Let's make a life together. With kids and a successful business." A brilliant smile bloomed. "We can have it all."

"We absolutely can." He brought his lips to hers. "And we will."

* * * * *

Look for the next book in the
Texas Cattleman's Club: Heir Apparent series:

Bidding on a Texan *by Barbara Dunlop*

COMING NEXT MONTH FROM

ⓗ HARLEQUIN
DESIRE

#2827 RANCHER'S CHRISTMAS STORM
Gold Valley Vineyards • by Maisey Yates
Things have been tense since rancher Jericho Smith's most recent
acquisition—Honey Cooper's family winery. What she thought was her
inheritance now belongs to her brother's infuriatingly handsome best
friend. But when they're forced together during a snowstorm, there's no
escaping the heat between them...

#2828 BIDDING ON A TEXAN
Texas Cattleman's Club: Heir Apparent
by Barbara Dunlop
To save their families' reputations and fortunes, heiress Gina Edmonds and
hardworking business owner Rafe Cortez-Williams reluctantly team up for
a cowboy bachelor auction. Their time together reveals an undeniable
attraction, but old secrets may derail everything they hope to build...

#2829 THE EX UPSTAIRS
Dynasties: The Carey Center • by Maureen Child
A decade ago, Henry Porter spent one hot night with Amanda Carey
before parting on bad terms. They're both powerful executives now, and
he's intentionally bought property she needs. To find out why, Amanda
goes undercover as his new maid, only to be tempted by him again...

#2830 JUST A LITTLE MARRIED
Moonlight Ridge • by Reese Ryan
To claim her inheritance, philanthropist Riley George makes a marriage
deal with the celebrity chef catering her gala, Travis Holloway—who's also
her ex. Needing the capital for his family's resort, Travis agrees. It's strictly
business until renewed sparks and long-held secrets threaten everything...

#2831 A VERY INTIMATE TAKEOVER
Devereaux Inc. • by LaQuette
Once looking to take him down, Trey Devereaux must now band
together with rival Jeremiah Benton against an even larger corporate
threat. But as tensions grow, so does the fire between them. When
secrets come to light, can they save the company *and* their relationship?

#2832 WHAT HAPPENS AT CHRISTMAS...
Clashing Birthrights • by Yvonne Lindsay
As CEO Kristin Richmond recovers from a scandal that rocked her family's
business, a new threat forces her to work with attorney Hudson Jones,
who just happens to be the ex who left her brokenhearted. But Christmas
brings people together...especially when there's chemistry!

**YOU CAN FIND MORE INFORMATION ON UPCOMING HARLEQUIN TITLES,
FREE EXCERPTS AND MORE AT HARLEQUIN.COM.**

HDCNM0921

SPECIAL EXCERPT FROM

⒣ HARLEQUIN
DESIRE

*Things have been tense since rancher Jericho Smith's
most recent acquisition—Honey Cooper's family winery.
What she thought was her inheritance now belongs
to her brother's ridiculously handsome best friend.
But when they're forced together during a snowstorm,
there's no escaping the heat between them...*

Read on for a sneak peek at
Rancher's Christmas Storm
by New York Times *bestselling author Maisey Yates!*

"Maybe you could stay." Her voice felt scratchy; she
felt scratchy. Her heart was pounding so hard she could
barely hear, and the steam filling up the room seemed to
swallow her voice.

But she could see Jericho's face. She could see the
tightness there. The intensity.

"Honey..."

"No. I just... Maybe this is the time to have a
conversation, actually. The one that we decided to have
later. Because I'm getting warm. I'm very warm."

"Put your robe back on."

"What if I don't want to?"

"Why not?"

"Because I want you. I already admitted to that. Why
do you think I'm so upset? All the time? About all the
women that you bring into the winery, about the fact that

my father gave it to you. About the fact that we're stuck together, but will never actually be together. And that's why I had to leave. I'm not an idiot, Jericho. I know that you and I are never going to… We're not going to fall in love and get married. We can hardly stand to be in the same room as each other.

"But I have wanted you since I understood what that meant. And I don't know what to do about it. Short of running away and having sex with someone else. That was my game plan. My game plan was to go off and have sex with another man. And that got thwarted. You were the one that picked me up. You're the one that I'm stuck here with in the snow. And I'm not going to claim that it's fate. Because I can feel myself twisting every single element of this except for the weather. The blizzard isn't my fault. But I'm making the choice to go ahead and offer…me."

"I…"

"If you're going to reject me, just don't do it horribly."

And then suddenly she found herself being tugged into his arms, the heat from his body more intense than the heat from the sauna, the roughness of his clothes a shock against her skin. And then his mouth crashed down on hers.

Don't miss what happens next in…
Rancher's Christmas Storm
by New York Times *bestselling author Maisey Yates!*

Available October 2021 wherever
Harlequin Desire books and ebooks are sold.

Harlequin.com

Return to Jackson Falls for the next sexy and irresistible book in Synithia Williams's reader-favorite series featuring the Robidoux family!

It's been three years since she walked away from him— and made the biggest mistake of her life. But when they're forced to work together, that old flame burns hotter than ever. Can they find a second chance with their first love?

Read on for a sneak peek at
Foolish Hearts

Ashiya pushed open the door to the clubhouse at the same time someone pulled from the other side. She lost her balance and stumbled forward on her high heels. She barely stopped herself from falling forward. A warm hand reached out and steadied her by the elbow.

"Excuse me."

"Sorry," a familiar male voice said at the same time.

Ashiya froze. The blood rushed from her face and her lungs decided breathing wasn't necessary at that moment. Her eyes jerked up. Surprise, embarrassment and regret sent her body into a confusing tailspin. Russell seemed just as surprised to see her. Her heart squeezed while the lingering touch of his hand on her elbow turned her limbs into jelly.

Russell. The-guy-she-should-have-chosen Russell. Fine-as-hell Russell. He would be the person she saw right now when she was already discombobulated.

Fine as hell was a weak string of words to describe Russell Gilchrist. Tall, broad of shoulders, thick of thighs and sweet of heart, Russell was the perfect embodiment of good guy with just a hint of bad boy beneath to make a woman fantasize about seeing him lose control. The lights from outside the clubhouse added a silvery glow to his sandy-brown skin and brought out the gold in his hazel eyes. He'd offered her everything she'd said she wanted in a relationship, and in turn she'd broken his heart when the jerk came back and said all the right words with wrong intentions.

After recognition entered his gaze, he quickly snatched his hand back. "You good?" His voice had lost the concern from before he'd recognized her. Instead it was cold, clipped as if he couldn't wait to get away from her.

Don't miss what happens next in...
Foolish Hearts *by Synithia Williams,*
available September 2021 wherever
HQN books and ebooks are sold.

HQNBooks.com